A Study In Statecraft
The Political Memoirs Of Mycroft Holmes

The Redacted Sherlock Holmes

The Novels II

Orlando Pearson

Hardcover ISBN 978-1-80424-276-6
Paperback ISBN 978-1-80424-277-3
ePub ISBN 978-1-80424-278-0
PDF ISBN 978-1-80424-279-7

Published by MX Publishing
335 Princess Park Manor, Royal Drive,
London, N11 3GX
www.mxpublishing.co.uk

Cover design Brian Belanger

Contents

**Introduction by Henry Durham, historical advisor to the
Redacted Sherlock Holmes series**

My discovery of the papers of Dr Watson at the Public Record
Office at Kew in the summer of 2015 created a frisson of
excitement among historians of the exploits of Dr Watson's
companion, Sherlock Holmes, as well as among historians in the
wider sense.

Here, as set out in the books published as *The Redacted Sherlock
Holmes*, we learned of matters that were too scandalous to publish
in the lifetime of the Great Baker Street Detective. For the first
time the true and somewhat tawdry reason for the flight of
Hitler's deputy Rudolph Hess to Scotland in 1941 was revealed,
as well as the Victorian response to incipient climate change, and
the real killer of a famous Scottish king. Alongside many other
personal details, we also learned of Sherlock Holmes's musical
French sister, the eminent French composer or *composatrice*
Augusta Holmès, and of his famous German grandson, Gottfried
von Cramm, one of the top tennis players in the world in the
1930s.

In Dr Watson's papers, it was striking how often Mycroft
Holmes, Sherlock's brother, who only appears twice in the
canonical accounts of Sherlock Holmes's activities, figured when
matters of state were involved. The process of editing and
releasing Dr Watson's papers, which has been continuing since
2015, is still far from complete, but, as a historical researcher, I
cast my net widely, and I have been preoccupied with work in
other areas.

One of these is 19th century sporting history. It was in the summer of 2023, while doing some research into Derbyshire County Cricket Club and, in particular, into two of the stalwarts of the Derbyshire team in the 1880s, the half-brothers Thomas and William Mycroft, that I made a life-changing discovery.

For, filed, or misfiled, amongst records of the cricketing exploits of the Mycroft brothers, were the private papers of Mycroft Holmes.

Further research revealed that they had been maintained by Dr Watson, who sometimes (but as we shall see, by no means always) acts as Mycroft's narrator. They were passed to Orlando Pearson, Dr Watson's successor as Sherlock Holmes's assistant and chronicler, and then passed back to the Watson family, before being deposited at the Public Record Office in 1990 by the literary executors of Dr Watson's son, Edward, after the latter's death. The works behind the original *Redacted Sherlock Holmes* series have the same complex process of transmission although they had not suffered the same misfiling as these papers of Mycroft Holmes which the purest chance has brought to light after being for so long lost.

So what did we know of Mycroft Holmes before the dramatic rediscovery of these papers?

Most of it comes from the two canonical stories in which he appears – the undated though early *Greek Interpreter* and *The Bruce Partington Plans* of 1895. His brother Sherlock is more candid about his brother in the latter, and I make no apology for quoting at length from the latter work as he tells Watson about him.

One has to be discreet when one talks of high matters of state. You are right in thinking that he is under the British government. You would also be right in a sense if you said that occasionally he IS the British government."

"My dear Holmes!"

"I thought I might surprise you. Mycroft draws four hundred and fifty pounds a year (*Editorial note*: about £45,000 or USD 55,000 in 2023's money), remains a subordinate, has no ambitions of any kind, will receive neither honour nor title, but remains the most indispensable man in the country."

"But how?"

"Well, his position is unique. He has made it for himself. There has never been anything like it before, nor will be again. He has the tidiest and most orderly brain, with the greatest capacity for storing facts, of any man living. The same great powers which I have turned to the detection of crime he has used for this particular business. The conclusions of every department are passed to him, and he is the central exchange, the clearing house, which makes out the balance. All other men are specialists, but his specialism is omniscience....In that great brain of his everything is pigeon-holed and can be handed out in an instant. Again and again his word has decided the national policy. He lives in it. He thinks of nothing else."

In *The Greek Interpreter* we had learnt that Mycroft Holmes is seven years older than his brother which would mean he was born in 1847. As the Holmes family were country squires, it is likely that there was a brother older than Mycroft who looked after the family estate while the younger brothers, Mycroft and Sherlock, were expected to make their own ways in the world, and being a senior civil servant (although not being a consulting detective) was one of the standard ways of doing so. Other than that, we learn of his obese appearance in *The Bruce Partington Plans* – Mycroft's bloated figure features also in *A Modern Odysseus* in this work – and of his skill as an observer and as a maker of inferences, where he is more acute than his brother. But beyond this we had known little about him before his papers were rediscovered.

In fact, besides providing much welcome detail about Mycroft's career, these papers confirm many of the things that his brother said of Mycroft in *The Greek Interpreter*. Mycroft had bachelor quarters in Pall Mall and was a member of the Diogenes Club, the peculiar club in St James's Street where members were not permitted to take the least notice of each other and talking was banned except in the Stranger's Room. These peculiarities of the Diogenes Club play an important role, as the reader will discover, in *A Goat in the Government*. There is no fellow lodger for Mycroft, unlike Sherlock, who, with intermissions, shared quarters with Dr Watson for many years. Mycroft mentions no outside interests, whereas his brother was a noted chemist and musician. There is not even a mention of a landlord or landlady for Mycroft, although it is hard to believe that a man of his social class should have had no servants at all and hence did his own chores.

I have arranged the matters I have chosen to set before the public in this volume in chronological order.

The first details his dealings with George Goschen, who was British Chancellor of Exchequer (the equivalent of Secretary to the Treasury in the United States) at the time of the disappearance of Sherlock Holmes, in 1891. By the time of the second story in 1914, Mycroft Holmes had gone up a level in seniority, as the main political figure he deals with is the Prime Minister, Herbert Asquith. Asquith was replaced as Prime Minister by David Lloyd George in December 1916, and in the third and fourth events covered, Mycroft Holmes is his chief advisor. As detailed at the conclusion of this fourth matter, Mycroft Holmes fell out of favour with Lloyd George, and took a less prominent role in the years that followed. But *The Royal Bachelor* (how appropriate that Sherlock Holmes should have had to make do with a bachelor from the British nobility in *The Noble Bachelor* while Mycroft gets to hobnob with royalty!) sees Mycroft Holmes back in service assisting Prime Minister Stanley Baldwin in the Abdication Crisis of 1936. It is noticeable that while Goschen, Asquith, and Lloyd George all came from the Liberal Party, Baldwin was from the Conservatives, which suggests that politicians regardless of party had no reservation about making use of Mycroft's unique political skills.

And what can we make of Mycroft Holmes from these newly unearthed documents?

As the only man who could go toe to toe with Sherlock Holmes when it came to observation and inference, Mycroft Holmes was in a unique position to comment on the much better-known detective work of his brother. There is an example of this in *The Greek Interpreter* where Mycroft Holmes said of his brother:

By the way, Sherlock, I expected to see you round last week, to consult me over that Manor House case. I thought you might be a little out of your depth.

In the episodes in this collection, Mycroft shows himself to be the equal of his brother at investigative work where such work does not require him "to run here and run there, to cross-question railway guards, and lie on my face with a lens to my eye" as he states in *The Bruce-Partington Plans*. Mycroft obviously likes this quotation about his own limitations as it appears at the head of the first episode of these memoirs and it is notable that in the matters presented here, Mycroft (writing in the confident expectation that what he wrote would not be read in his own lifetime) is often even more slighting of the abilities of his brother than he is in the quotation about the Manor House case above.

The events that follow have a mix of narrative voices.

An Individual of High Net Worth (May 1891) is largely recounted by Dr Watson at the time of the Great Hiatus (from April 1891 to April 1894), while *A Modern Odysseus* (June 1914) is told entirely by Mycroft although his brother Sherlock features. *A Goat in the Government* (May 1918) and *The Art of the Possible* (November 1918), have Mycroft and Watson each give part of the account of events, and Sherlock Holmes does some characteristically smart detective work in the former case. *The Royal Bachelor* of December 1936 has Mycroft act both as narrator and as prime mover although Sherlock Holmes and Dr Watson appear in a brief scene retold by the latter.

And what of the statecraft which is presented here?

Mycroft makes it clear that his aim is to write a political handbook and these memoirs would probably not be associated with detective fiction at all if they had not been compiled by the brother of Sherlock Holmes. Mycroft is described in these memoirs as the Prime Minister's Permanent Special Advisor, and his span in this role coincides with the time when the Almighty had made this land of hope and glory as mighty as it has ever been to date. As noted above, Mycroft Holmes's eminence was at the disposal of politicians regardless of political allegiance and, as *The Royal Bachelor* points out, nearly a quarter of this planet's population at the time covered by these memoirs had the good fortune to be governed by the British.

It is for the reader to decide whether it is a matter of chance that this apogee of British power and influence was at the same time as the apogee of the influence and power of Mycroft Holmes.

London 2023

FOREWORD

by Mycroft Holmes

"Why do you not solve it yourself, Mycroft? You can see as far as I."

"Possibly, Sherlock. But it is a question of getting details. Give me your details, and from an armchair I will return you an excellent expert opinion. But to run here and run there, to cross-question railway guards, and lie on my face with a lens to my eye – it is not my *métier*."

THE BRUCE-PARTINGTON PLANS

So, what of my own investigations?

Readers of the accounts made by the Dr Watson of the cases conducted by my brother Sherlock, who is somewhat less unintelligent but in other ways almost as limited as the good Doctor, have wondered this.

The book that follows provides the answer as it sets out accounts of some of the matters in which I played a leading role. These were not in the forensic area of crime but in the broader world of statecraft, which is a separate specialism in most, though not all, cases. In compiling this work, it was irritatingly hard not to follow Dr Watson's narrative technique of presenting each matter as a mystery requiring a solution. It pains me to have to stoop to Dr Watson's level, but my reader will discover that my investigations are of far greater moment than those of my brother which Dr Watson quotes me as describing as "the petty puzzles of the police court".

And why this work at all?

I feel that Dr Watson has given my younger brother more than his share of the palms and it is time that my role as the prime mover behind the British government's statecraft which has led to this country being the greatest power the world has ever seen receives its due. As my brother has put it in one his rare insightful remarks, "Crime is common, but logic is rare." And logic at the level I apply it and its application in the field in which I operate, is rarer still, and so needs a work to celebrate it.

And why the structure as this work is a series of episodes which illustrate my skills? Sometimes I confine myself to saying what was happening and how my counsel turned events to my country's advantage. At other times I show my engagement in the most complex matters facing our generation. I feel that presenting my victories in this form show that the best movers in statecraft are not those who solve matters once they have become problematic, but those who prevent matters becoming problematic in the first place. I see it, therefore, as my role not to step in like some *deus ex machina* or divine power to solve things when the chips are down, but rather to make sure the chips always stay up.

But I get ahead of myself.

The trifling matter described in the episode that follows – *An Individual of High Net Worth* – is one of those mysteries which Dr Watson brought to my attention while my brother was missing assumed dead, although, as my reader may observe from the opening remarks in what the doctor writes, it must have been obvious that there was something more than a little curious about my brother's apparent death. Accordingly, Sherlock does not appear in it at all, and I solve not only the intellectual puzzle that Dr Watson brought to my attention, but also facilitate the political resolution of the matters raised.

At the conclusion of events, I asked Dr Watson for his notes and embargoed their publication as I would not wish the workings of statecraft to become public knowledge until long after my time at this country's helm has come to an end.

EPISODE I

An Individual of High Net Worth

by Dr John Watson

So here I was, once more back at Baker Street.

Since my return from Switzerland after the death of my friend, Sherlock Holmes, I had been here often. It was all so recent – the unexpected arrival of Sherlock Holmes in my consulting room, his precipitate departure over the backwall of the garden, our vain flight to the Continent, and his disappearance into the abyss of the Reichenbach Falls leaving me bereft even of a body to mourn. Sometimes I could hear the roar of the torrent in my head, and sometimes, like today, I fancied I could hear Holmes calling to me through the misty spray.

So here it was that I had come to grieve. And grieving was made all the harder by the fact that my friend's brother, Mycroft Holmes (whom I shall normally refer to by his first name to avoid confusion with Sherlock Holmes), had placed an embargo on any published mention of my friend's death.

"The whole matter," he murmured with an airiness which betrayed a detachment that I was completely unable to share, "is *sub judice* and may not be given any publicity until the trial of Moriarty's associates is complete. And, given the speed with which the wheels of justice, as so much else, turn in this country, that is likely to remain the case for several years to come. And indeed, Dr Watson," continued he, with a sudden earnestness that was entirely uncharacteristic of his normally dispassionate persona, "I cannot impress on you enough the importance of keeping the fate of my brother a secret until I say you are able to refer to it."

So it was that distribution of the *Journal de Genève* of the 6th of May 1891 which contained an account of my friend's death was barred in this country, and that the Reuters' despatch covering the same events for the English papers on the 7th of May was withheld from publication. It was only when Moriarty's brother, James, wrote to the English press with his own perverse version of events, that Mycroft sanctioned the publication of *The Final Problem* in December 1893.

This meant that there was no one apart from my fair wife, Mary, whom I had telegrammed from Switzerland with the news of Holmes's death, with whom I was able to speak. For my own part, I fell into the deepest melancholy when I returned from Switzerland, extremely reluctant to go out anywhere, almost incapable of seeing patients in my surgery, and consequently unable to earn a living from my medical practice.

It was not as though my outgoings had ceased.

I have dwelt elsewhere on the home-centred interests which rise up around the man who finds himself master of his own establishment. While these home-centred interests had brought me great happiness, they came with significant financial cost, and, as my outgoings remained the same after my return from Switzerland, so I found debts mounted as my income declined.

The only place I could find any sense of solace was at the flat in Baker Street where I now found myself and to which I repaired whenever I could even though it was well over three years since I had lived here.

On my visits, Mrs Hudson would open the door to the first-floor sitting-rom, the only place on earth that offered a sanctuary for my troubled mind.

And there they all still were!

The Persian slipper, the pipes by the hearth, the violin in its case by the chair where my friend normally sat, and the chemistry equipment at the table in our sitting-room at which we had eaten. The mementoes of my time of happiness.

"See Dr Watson," said Mrs Hudson, as though reading my thoughts, "I've left Mr Holmes's things here. I shall not be moving them for some little time until..." she broke off and looked away, and my heart quickened just a little. Could Mrs Hudson know something different from what all the evidence pointed to about the disappearance of my friend? But, rather than giving me anything on which I might pin a hope, Mrs Hudson continued in a matter-of-fact way, "...my planning application has come through."

"Your planning application?" I asked, although my thoughts were elsewhere. "What are you planning?"

"Yes," said she. "I am applying to turn this room into a place where local mothers of babes and nurslings can leave their charges when they go to work. That may take a while though. Getting the authorities to agree to anything is so slow. My daughter, Mrs Turner, she…" Mrs Hudson carried on talking about her plans to set up a children's nursery, but I was far too overwrought to take in what she said.

Alongside the normal sights of Baker Street there was also the correspondence. Someone – Mrs Hudson, I assumed – had secured it to the mantelpiece by a jack-knife in the time-honoured manner of my late friend.

Ah yes, the correspondence.

It still came flooding in with every one of the day's seven postal deliveries.

The excuse I had given to dear Mary for my visits to Baker Street was that I needed to see whether any mail addressed to me had been delivered there, even though, after I had left Baker Street on our marriage, I had never bothered to go back to check. But Mycroft had also asked me to review any mail that arrived at Baker Street addressed to his brother. "And feel free," he had added, "to raise with me any matter that arises from it where you feel you are overtasked to deal with it yourself. I will be somewhat surprised if I do not hear from you quite often." And so, I claimed a double justification for my visit even though no one, I think, was under any illusion that I was there for any other reason than to come to terms with the loss of my friend.

As might be expected, there was always much more mail at Baker Street for Sherlock Holmes than the few items – mainly medical circulars from journals which I had not thought to tell of the changes in my living arrangements – that were addressed for me. I took my place in the familiar seat by the fire-place to review what was quite a pile which I placed on my lap. The grate was empty for it was mid-May, the weather was glorious, and the sun shone mockingly through the window.

Among the pile, one missive caught my attention. It was in a stiff manilla envelope, addressed to Mr Sherlock Holmes, and, when I opened it, was hand-written on note paper of the most fashionable quality.1 May, 1891

Fairbanks

Streatham

1 May,1891

Dear Mr Holmes,

You will remember me from the case to which your biographer, Dr Watson, applied the title, *The Beryl Coronet.*

As you will doubtless recall, a prominent person, whom Dr Watson had the good sense not to identify in his published account of events, borrowed £50,000 from the bank, Holder and Stevenson, of which I am one of the two senior partners. The eminent, indeed illustrious, borrower did so against the security of the coronet of the story's title. For my part, I was by no means convinced of his right to use as a pledge what I described at the time as one of the most precious possessions of the Empire, as, almost by definition, this description of it excluded the possibility that the coronet could have been the property of the man who was seeking to borrow from my bank. I confess that I made a monumental error when I let my desire to make a swift turn overcame my natural prudence in making an advance.

I am writing to you now as I have been asked to advance money in circumstances that are similarly obscure and, based on my experience with the beryl coronet, I thought it wise to seek your advice before I did so. As this is a private letter the contents of which I am relying on your good sense not to publicise, I am prepared to disclose the name of the would-be borrower.

Mr Geoffrey Beddows will be a name well-known to you. He is the founder of Hammerson Ltd. He remains a major shareholder and managing director of the company which supplies goods of all sorts direct to homes across the country and beyond. Mr Beddows saw the opportunity provided by advances in telegram services and in the even more recently developed telephone to communicate directly with the general public, whose members can now place orders for goods by these new means of communication for delivery straight to their door in a time-scale that is bewilderingly short. Although he has other business interests, Beddows remains Hammerson's managing director. The company was founded no more than a score of years ago and yet is already amongst the largest concerns in the land with delivery offices in every town.

"Mr Holder," said Mr Beddows, when the attendant who had ushered him into my office had taken his leave, "I have been informed that you are in the habit of advancing money."

"The firm does so when the security is good," I answered cautiously.

"It is absolutely essential to me," he continued, "that I should have £50,000 at once."

"I should be happy to advance it without further parley from my own private purse," said I, "were it not that the strain would be rather more than it could bear."

I confess that, having had my fingers more than a little burnt with the beryl coronet, I was more cautious on my own financial means than I strictly needed to be, but I am sure you will understand my situation.

"If, on the other hand," I continued, "I am to make the advance in the name of the firm, then in justice to my partner I must insist that, even in your case, every business-like precaution should be taken. And irrespective of what you and I agree here, I will have to confirm so significant an advance before it is made with my partner who is absent at present."

"I am happy to provide as security shares of Hammerson Ltd held in my own name to a value of any reasonable multiple of the amount I borrow that you might care to stipulate."

"That sounds to me more than adequate," I responded, relieved after my experience described in *The Beryl Coronet* that my debtor was offering to provide security to which his title was indisputable and whose value could be readily ascertained. "For an advance of that size backed by security such as that, the firm will charge you interest at half a per cent above that charged by the Bank of England – that stands at three and a half per cent per annum at present so we would charge you four per cent."

"I am pleased that this is being treated as an entirely arm's length transaction," replied Mr Beddows.

"And when will you repay the money?" I asked.

Although this was, I thought in the circumstances, an entirely professional question, for the first time a look of some uncertainty flitted over the face of my would-be debtor, and I feared he would name some repayment date, which, for whatever reason, lay far in the future.

Instead, after a long pause, Mr Beddows, "I am happy for the loan to be repayable on demand at any time."

I could not see why Mr Beddows should need a loan of this size if it were to be repayable on demand and I put this to him.

"Mr Holder," said Beddows, his previous assurance returning, "with the security I am offering, I could get a loan from anyone in the country so I could get someone else to advance me money to replace this debt just as you can. Thus, the risk to you of not recovering your money is negligible."

"So, when do you propose actually to repay the money?" I asked in some confusion.

"As I stated, whenever you wish me to," replied he, with, what to my heightened senses came across as an air of evasiveness, "although, obviously, interest will stop accruing to you when the loan is repaid."

"So, you want the loan to be repayable on demand. But surely you must have some plan for making payments to finance the debt, even if they only represent the interest that has accrued on the outstanding amount," I persisted.

"Mr Holder, you have a loan which is repayable on demand, you may accrue interest on the loan at the rate we agree, and you have as security assets the value of which you can track every day through the financial press. Sovereign states issue debt with no redemption date – the debt taken out to finance this country's efforts in the Napoleonic

Wars more than half a century ago is still outstanding – and I do not see why I should be subject to any different arrangements."

"You are not a sovereign state, Mr Beddows…" I rejoindered.

"Indeed not, Mr Holder," shot back Mr Beddows, "My creditworthiness is much better than that of most sovereign states…"

"And this country pays interest on its outstanding debt for the Napoleonic Wars."

"As for your trifling concerns about payment, you may endorse the debt to anyone else you may wish at any time if you want to crystallise the amount I owe you. And if the market value of the shares serving as your security falls below the value of the amount outstanding, I will provide you with more shares to take the value of the security up to what is owed."

"Very well, Mr Beddows," replied I after some consideration, "as I have stated, for so significant a sum I will have to put the matter to my partner, Mr Stevenson, on his return. And I will also have to disclose to him the repayment arrangements or the lack of them."

"I should much prefer that you did so," said he. "I would not wish to have any special terms extended to me or to create any sort of business relationship that is out of the ordinary."

I forbore to mention that the arrangement under discussion was as out of the ordinary as loan against the security of the beryl coronet. Instead, I confined myself to saying, "I look forward to reverting to you shortly. You will understand the reason why I cannot advance you funds without the matter receiving further discussion," as I bowed Mr Beddows out.

After he had gone, I considered my position. Mr Beddows's proposition offered the bank no ostensible risk and yet to advance him money when he appears to have no clear plan – indeed no plan at all - to repay it does not seem to be a business proposition.

I would welcome your thoughts on this matter and look forward to hearing from you.

Your sincerely,

Alexander Holder

When I had first seen Mr Holder five years earlier as he dashed up Baker Street from the Metropolitan Line station at the junction with the Marylebone Road, I had said to Holmes that it looked like a madman was on the loose. This letter did at least suggest that he had learnt some caution in his business dealings, and I was still turning the matter he had addressed to Holmes over in my head when I heard the sound of footsteps on the stairs and the buttons put his head round the door.

"Dr Watson, there's a Mr Alexander Holder to see Mr Holmes. I told him Mr Holmes was not in and that I did not know when he would come back but Mr Holder would not be put off. In the end,

I told him that you were here, and he said, 'Well, If I can't see Mr Holmes, I will have to make do with Dr Watson.'"

Mr Alexander Holder

Portrait by Sidney Paget from the time of *The Beryl Cornet*

"Then you had better show him up," said I with a sigh, "and I will see what I can do to help him."

By 1891, Mr Holder was a man of about fifty-five. He was still tall, even portlier than at the time of *The Beryl Coronet* whence this picture of him comes, but imposing, with a massive, strongly marked face, and a commanding figure. He was dressed in a sombre yet rich style, in black frock-coat, shining hat, neat brown gaiters, and well-cut pearl-grey trousers.

"I see you have read my letter, Dr Watson," said he, glancing at the piece of paper which I had laid on the table in front of me. "I confess I had hoped that it would receive the attention of Mr Sherlock Holmes."

"Mr Holmes," I said, trying hard to suppress any emotion in my voice, "is away at present. His return is not anticipated at any time that is at present foreseeable."

"And what did you make of the contents of my letter?"

"It is certainly a most mysterious matter," I replied cautiously. "I really wish that Mr Holmes were here to give his opinion," I added with some feeling. "May I ask why you have now come round here when one of the few things I know about the current activities of Mr Holmes is that he will not yet have had the opportunity to reply to you."

"There have been some developments in the matter which I wanted to raise with Mr Holmes but which I trust you will be able to raise with him on my behalf when he returns."

This latest sally placed me in an invidious position but in the end I said, "I will do whatever I can to help," with as much sincerity as I could muster. "Perhaps you would care to set out to me what it is you would wish to convey to Mr Holmes."

"When my partner, Mr Stevenson, returned to the office," replied Holder, "I put Beddows's request to him at our first meeting."

"And what was his response?" asked I.

"I found that Mr Stevenson had already advanced Beddows the money he wanted from his own personal funds."

"He had already transacted business on his own behalf which might have gone to your partnership?"

"That is so. I put this to Mr Stevenson who replied, with some froideur, 'You have expressed your own misgivings about Mr Beddows's proposition, and, by your own word, you too had considered transacting with him on your own account. All I did was to give effect to what you considered doing yourself. And doing business on my own account rather than through our partnership is permitted by our partnership agreement.'"

"Does that not mean," asked I, intrigued, like Holmes's would-be petitioner, why a man of the wealth of Mr Beddows should be seeking to borrow money at all let alone on these strange terms, "that Mr Beddows must have spoken to your partner and received funds from him even before he came to see you to seek a loan."

"That is also the case," replaced Mr Holder. "I made the same point to Stevenson who shrugged and said, 'This is a private matter between Mr Beddows and me, and I am not obliged to tell you anything. But, for your information, I need not know why Mr Beddows wants to borrow money, nor why he has asked for the loan to be subject to the conditions that he has asked for, nor whom else he has asked for an advance. I need only decide whether the payment terms are acceptable to me and whether the security he has provided is adequate.'"

"Is that all he said?" I asked, my curiosity mounting.

"Mr Stevenson went on, 'I took the view I could live with the terms Mr Beddows has asked for, and he has given me a signed transfer document that I can use to transfer the shares into my ownership to the value of the amount outstanding should he at any time seem unable to repay his loan. The shares themselves are in my private safe. I have the right to demand repayment with interest at any time, and I can endorse the debt to another party if I so choose. That Mr Beddows should also have sought a loan from the bank or from you personally is not my concern as my own position is entirely secure.'"

I digested this very long deposition and wished more than ever that it were Holmes who was conducting this consultation with Mr Holder. In the end, to satisfy myself that I had understood the gravamen of Mr Holder's deposition, I summarised it back to him.

"So, your colleague Mr Stevenson has lent £50,000 to Mr Beddows with no repayment plan of any sort but Mr Stevenson has as security shares in Mr Beddows's company. He can recover the debt at any time by enforcing the security and he can also endorse the debt to any third party at any time of his choice. He has transacted this business on his own account. Even though Mr Beddows is already in receipt of funds from your partner, he has separately approached you to make a similar advance on the same terms either from the bank or on your own account."

"That is the matter in a nutshell, Dr Watson."

"And I take it that you have not yet responded to Mr Beddows's request to you."

"I concluded following my discussions with Mr Stevenson that I would not be able to make an advance from the funds of our banking partnership. But if Mr Stevenson feels the security he has from Mr Beddows is sufficient to make a personal advance, then maybe I could make an advance to Mr Beddows at a higher rate and make a turn on my own account. And that is why I came to see your colleague, Mr Sherlock Holmes."

"And what would you like Mr Holmes to do?" I said, trusting that my quavering voice would not betray my insincerity in posing this question.

"Mr Holmes's investigative skills are quite unparalleled and his opinion on the wisdom of making such an advance would set my mind greatly at rest. I confess that I wish I had adopted the same course of action before I advanced money against the security of the beryl coronet."

"I will do whatever I can," I said, choosing my words with great circumspection, "to convey your disquisition to Mr Holmes. But I regret that cannot undertake to give you a precise date when I might have a response."

Mr Holder thanked me for my offer with a sincerity that in the circumstances I found disconcerting and went on his way, while I contemplated what further steps, if any, I might take.

In Holmes's absence – as I thought *sine die* – it struck me that I could at least put myself in Mr Holder's shoes and perform the due diligence which Mr Holder, in retrospect, might have carried out for himself.

The easiest place to start, I thought, would be the public accounts of Hammerson Limited published in the *London Gazette* and I betook myself to the London Library to review these. When I got hold of them, I was unsurprised to note that they disclosed a storming financial performance by the company in the year ended 30th of September 1889, the most recent year for which figures were available, and suggesting glittering prospects for the business in the years ahead.

The annual report also revealed the number of shares – one million – that Mr Beddows held in the business.

As I considered my reasoning, I felt a pressing need for more cigarettes than my case contained and, when at the tobacconist, I took the opportunity to buy *The Times* which disclosed the current share price of Hammerson. At fourteen shillings and two pence per share, it stood at an all-time high and multiplied by the one million shares held by Mr Beddows, meant that the value of his holding stood at just over £700,000. This is much the same size as the value of Baskerville estate had been in 1889 and Holmes had commented then that for so gigantic a sum a man might play a dangerous game. His shareholding alone made Mr Beddows one of the richest men on the planet and the report also disclosed his annual salary which stood at no less than £100,000 – this is more than eighty times more than what the Prime

Minister earns. Mr Beddows, I mused, was probably understating the situation when he said that his creditworthiness was better than that of many a sovereign state.

Having read these eye-watering numbers and considered what they told me about Mr Beddows, I then spent some time examining the library's array of the output from the financial press. I saw that at the company's annual general meeting in the previous year, outside shareholders had expressed what was variously described as concern and as outrage, that the managing director was awarding himself such a large share of the company's success. Mr Beddows's airy response had been, "It was I who saw the opportunity to create the company's success in the first place and it was I who put the measures in place to make the most of the opportunity. Accordingly, it is my view that I should receive a due reward for my foresightedness. As a result of it we have millions of customers counting on us at Hammerson. And I have thousands of investors counting on us. And any rewards that I reap are closely linked to the performance of Hammerson."

I sat and contemplated the conflicting nature of the public and private information I had. In the end, rather than going home, I returned to Baker Street – "What Dr Watson? Back again already?" I heard Mrs Hudson say as I went up the seventeen steps – hoping that its surroundings might inspire me while I considered matters. Mr Beddows, I reasoned, had an urgent and unexplained need for a large advance, and yet his wealth in shares on the data I had and his salary for the previous year must have made meeting his every conceivable financial need a trivial matter.

I turned this contradiction in my head over and over again, and only one explanation would occur to me.

All the press reports I read of Hammerson's delivery service sounded a warning that the success of his delivery business would render the high street shop obsolete. But, I reasoned, the fortunes of Hammerson Limited must in fact have taken a severe downturn since the year ended 30 September 1889, if Mr Beddows now had a sudden need for personal funds.

But I also knew – I had not spent so many years sharing quarters with Sherlock Holmes for nothing – that his first reaction to a conclusion as startling as this would be to look for flaws in the logic.

The accounts had been audited by that eminent firm of auditors, accountants, and tax advisers Messrs Rice, Waterman, Tupper. They had expressed an unqualified opinion on the truth and fairness of the view the accounts presented and who was I, a mere doctor, to pretend I could see any more than they could? But the accounts, though the latest available, were already more than a year old, and a further search of the financial press revealed that Hammerson was due to publish its next annual report in less than a week's time and this would provide me with more information about Mr Beddows's affairs. And, it struck me, if next week Hammerson was going to reveal a downturn in its fortunes, then that would explain Mr Beddows's sudden need for an advance as, given his comments at the previous year's annual general meeting, such a downturn would surely be reflected in a reduction in his emoluments.

Having satisfied myself that I could justify my opinion of the real reason why Mr Beddows might be in need of funds, I thought about how I might apply the information that I had.

It struck me that only Mr Stevenson, Mr Beddows, Mr Holder, and I were privy to the information that Mr Beddows was seeking a loan. How, I asked myself, might I turn this inside information to my own account? And, I reasoned, I owed Mr Holder no obligation as I had said I would not revert to him until I had obtained the opinion of Mr Sherlock Holmes, and I had no means of doing this.

It was this moment that I seemed to hear the crisp voice of my friend Mr Sherlock Holmes calling to me from who knew where. "See Watson, what you have learnt from me from those years of our association. You have observed that Mr Beddows of Hammerson Ltd is in need of money. And you can infer that his business was not as buoyant as the share-price indicated."

"Now," and it was another voice that said this, "you can turn that inference to your advantage, for just as Sherlock Holmes used his inferences to solve his cases, you can turn your own inferences into cash."

As I had noted from *The Times,* Hammerson's share price stood at an all-time high.

My regular readers will know of my taste for speculation in shares and in the turf. If Hammerson's accounts, as I had good reason to believe, were going to show a declining position when its results for the year ended 30th of September 1891 were announced next week, then that price would fall. Why not take out a so-called future contract to sell shares at a future date at the current price. And then buy the shares to fulfil the contract when the share price, as I anticipated, had fallen? Such a speculation, armed with the knowledge I had, could hardly fail to be profitable. And, it occurred to me, making money in this way was a good deal more agreeable than sitting in my surgery listening to my patients' apparently intractable problems.

Feeling much better than I had done for a while at finally having something positive to do, I bounded back down the stairs of Baker Street, and headed to my stockbrokers on Cheapside, where I took out the future contract on the terms I have described. I then repaired to my home in Kensington to await the publication of Hammerson's results, the fall in its share price, and the handsome profit when I sold those shares at their present all-time high price having bought them after what I anticipated to be a precipitous fall.

My reader will imagine my chagrin when the results published the next week showed Hammerson had again achieved record sales and profits. Much prominence was given in the press release to a change in Mr Beddows's remuneration. His salary had fallen from its previously princely level to a much more modest £1,000 – though it is worth pointing out, that is still at about the same level as the salary of the Prime Minister. Mr Beddows has also waived dividends on his earnings and in the annual report. He explained the reduction of his earnings from the business as follows:

"I am the servant of the shareholders. I therefore felt it was inappropriate for me to take any significant sum out of the business in either salary or dividends as I feel the money is best invested in the business's future rather than being paid out as direct remuneration to me. Other shareholders have been offered the option to take their dividends in the form of new shares, but I have waived my right to these as well. I no longer want to have to defend myself against charges of rewarding myself too generously. In the end this decision was an easy one."

The shares of Hammerson soared to a new all-time high.

Mr Beddows's waiver of most of his emoluments may, of course, have explained his need to borrow money but I now had to buy shares to cover the future contract I had taken out at the new all-time price of Hammerson's shares.

My word is my bond, but I had no means to cover the contract. With the same facility with which I had calculated Mr Beddows's net worth, I could see that my losses on my contract – I was relieved that I had not asked to supply more shares under it – stood at no less than four hundred and twelve pounds, eighteen shillings, and fourpence or a third of my practice's revenue in a good year.

I sent a cheque to my stockbroker to cover my losses, but I did so in the full knowledge that my available funds would not cover it when the cheque was presented at the bank. I also sent a plaintive note to Mycroft. But, as I waited for a response from him, I started to fear every knock on the door in case it was my creditors trying to get what I owed them.

In the end, when another knock came, and once more I heard the maid say to the caller, "Dr Watson is not seeing callers at the present," I fled, scrambling over the backwall into the garden of the house behind just as my friend Sherlock Holmes had done only a few short weeks before.

I hurried to Baker Street – where else? – even though I knew there was no help to be had there.

"I will not smoke in the sitting room if you are turning it into a nursery for children," I said to Mrs Hudson when I arrived.

She looked somewhat puzzled by this offer and wrinkled her brow. "Ah yes, the nursery. My application has been in the works for so long I had all but forgotten about it. That is not going to happen for some time so you may smoke in there if you wish."

She went downstairs and I was about to light up but no sooner had I heard Mrs Hudson reach the bottom of the stairs when the bell rang.

"I will not respond to callers, I have the brain fever!" cried I, but it was too late. A messenger came straight upstairs from street and cried through the closed door of the flat, "Urgent message for Dr Watson."

Mycroft Holmes Opines

Rather in the way my occasionally somewhat callow brother Sherlock sometimes did, the good Dr Watson wrote to tell me he had got rather out of his depth – in this case in a distinctly unwise share speculation.

Had the matter been one which required detailed investigation – as I noted in the foreword to this memoir, my focus is firmly on great matters of state rather than on minutiae of daily life – I would have been unwilling or indeed unable to help him. But, as the solution was rather trite and as Mr Beddows's scheme had a potential impact on the nation's finances that was severe, I was able to help the good doctor. I was swayed in this decision by the fact that I could see no advantage to Dr Watson being consigned to a debtor's prison which he would have no prospect of emerging from for all that his highly speculative investment was most imprudent.

I despatched my messenger to Dr Watson's house with a summons to come to come to the Treasury at Whitehall and I gave my messenger the instruction that if the good doctor could not be found at his home, then my messenger should go to Baker Street. I had paid Mrs Hudson a year's rent in advance to keep my brother's quarters as they were with the only proviso that she tell no one of the arrangement. I had furnished her with an excuse for not disposing of my brother's impedimenta although the good woman found herself hard-pressed to remember it. I thus knew that Dr Watson could hole himself up in Baker Street for as long as he wished.

Rather than myself revealing how I solved Dr Watson's problem, I provide below the notes that Dr Watson made of what followed in his own inimitable style.

An Individual of High Net Worth (continuation by Dr Watson)

A summons to Whitehall after my humblest of petitions to Mycroft Holmes felt rather like one of those dreaded appointments at the headmaster's study from my schooldays.

George Goschen
1831-1907

I was shown into a meeting-room where, sitting with Mycroft, was a man who was introduced to me as George Goschen, Chancellor of the Exchequer, and a comfortably framed man in his early sixties. "We will," said Mycroft, "shortly be joined by another person, but, for your benefit, good doctor, and for you too, Chancellor, although I am sure you will have no need for my explanation, I will elucidate the matter for you first."

Goschen merely nodded but I said, for once in this narrative with the utmost sincerity, "I am all ears," as I hoped against hope that my plea to Mycroft might find me a way out of my imbroglio.

"I think it is fair to say, Dr Watson, that the mess you have got yourself into shows that you might be better off directing your energies to your medical practice rather than to high finance."

This reproof only increased the forebodings I felt about how the rest of the meeting might proceed and I refrained from making any comment.

"Have you," asked Mycroft after a lengthy pause, "ever given any thought as to why entrepreneurs go into business?".

"To make profits and to draw emoluments," I responded after a moment's thought, wondering why Mycroft should have started with a question to which the answer was self-evident.

"The problem with profits and emoluments is that they attract taxation."

"But why would an entrepreneur set up a business, if not to make a profit. And that necessarily will mean that an amount has to be paid in tax."

"That is so," said Goschen, speaking up for the first time, and his voice betraying the same bafflement as I had felt at what still seemed like a trick question. "What is the point of setting up a business if not to claim the reward for its success for which the state will also seek its share?"

"What an entrepreneur really wants is a business model that generates cash rather than profit. A flow of cash is not taxed whereas a flow of profit is."

"But how can a business make cash and not profits?" asked Goschen and I in unison.

At that moment there was a discrete knock at the mahogany door, and a uniformed official announced the arrival of Mr Frederick Tupper, the suave senior partner of the renowned accounting firm Rice, Waterman, Tupper.

"So Mr Tupper," asked Mycroft, "to how many other business owners apart from Mr Beddows of Hammerson have you sold your tax-avoiding device of taking out loans secured on the companies they run rather than drawing a salary and dividends?"

I fancy Mr Tupper had not been expecting so precipitate an opening to the discussion and he said nothing.

"This device," continued Mycroft, "means that, while their companies remain profitable and the value of their holdings secures their borrowings, the managing directors pay no tax on the cash they raise on the security of their company's shares."

"I would have thought," said Mr Tupper cautiously, "that the government would want to encourage enterprise. Taxation discourages it and the scheme which I have recommended to Mr Beddows allows him to reap the fullest reward for his business acumen."

"If everyone availed himself of such a scheme, the government would have no revenue with which to do things which benefit the public such as defending this realm and extending its empire."

"There is surely a balance which must be struck between retaining high levels of tax which discourage enterprise and low levels of tax which may actually result in more revenue being raised for the causes to which you refer. Much research has indicated that reducing rates of taxation results in higher tax revenue. The scheme we are discussing has been recommended by my firm so far only to Mr Beddows – although I understand he has taken advantage of it – and it merely addresses the balance between the need to raise taxes and the need to encourage enterprise."

"The scheme Mr Beddows has adopted means that he pays less tax on each consecutive pound of what he receives than his typist pays on her weekly wage of seventeen shillings and sixpence."

"No one is obliged to pay more tax than is required by the law. And everyone is entitled to arrange their affairs to minimise their tax liabilities."

"But this scheme is only available to this country's wealthiest citizens as poorer people do not have assets to offer as security in exchange for these permanent loans or the means to engage top tax advisors such as yourselves."

"Governments make the laws, and we give our clients no encouragement to break them. But laws were made for man, not man for laws. What Mr Beddows has done is entirely legal. If the government wishes to stop it, it needs to bring forward legislation which makes this scheme impossible. Given the glacial speed at which anything the government seeks to do progresses, you might achieve that in two years – unless there is an election before then. And the publicity you would thereby give to the scheme, would encourage more high net worth individuals to try to use it for as long as it remains legal. I can only see my firm benefitting from such publicity."

"Are you challenging us," interrupted Goschen, speaking on his own for the first time, and sounding rather grumpy, "to bring in legislation to stop this practice?"

Mr Tupper made no response. Instead, he sat back and awaited while Goschen considered his next sally.

"Well," said the Chancellor at length, "we could, I suppose, always stop Rice, Waterman, Tupper from getting any government contracts if they propose tax-avoidance schemes which deprive the exchequer of revenue."

"You know as well as I do, Mr Goschen," replied Tupper serenely, "that there are only three other business practices in the country of the scale of Rice, Waterman, Tupper so between the four of us we get well over 90% of government contracts. For most such contracts, we have been brought in to clear up the mess left behind by another practice which is accordingly excluded from the tendering, and at least one of the other firms will have blotted its copy-book in some other way. Thus, even if we are banned from tendering for contracts, the government will still have to award us some. The last time we were banned from taking on government business, our share of government contracts won increased compared to the previous period."

We seemed to have reached an impasse.

"I wonder if a political solution might not be more suited to resolving this matter," said Mycroft reflectively. "I merely advise the government ministers, you understand. You will understand, advisers advise, ministers decide, and I do not make policy."

"And a political solution would mean that we could continue to market our tax planning instruments?" asked Tupper.

I could see Mr Goschen was unsure on how to respond, but Mycroft, as was already becoming clear to me, was not a man given to self-doubt in his manoeuvrings.

"As you say, Mr Tupper," murmured Mycroft eventually, "there is nothing to stop you doing so at present, but I do wonder if the whole issue of the remuneration and taxation of this country's entrepreneurs needs looking at."

The Chancellor nodded, although I am far from sure he knew where this was leading.

"We probably need," continued Mycroft blandly, "to set up a committee led by a figure of probity in industry to report to the government on suitable ways in which the leading lights of industry in this country might be rewarded, and also to identify abuses in the current system. The senior partner of a firm like yours that is a scion of the City of London, might be a suitable person to chair such a committee. And there might be a place in the House of Lords or a knighthood for some of the members of the committee at the end of it. I have always felt that the ermine-clad ranks of the members of the House of Lords would be improved by an injection of people with numeracy skills."

"I should certainly be happy to consider such a suggestion," said Tupper, his face suddenly wreathed in smiles, "It would be an honour for my profession."

"And of course," continued Mycroft, "it would be most unfortunate if it should emerge that your firm should have recommended methods of remuneration to the country's leading entrepreneurs that are subsequently deemed undesirable by the committee."

Tupper nodded but I was sure he was being brought round by Mycroft's proposition.

"Perhaps," mused Goschen out loud, "Mr Beddows might be persuaded that a donation to our party would be a good use of his new additional wealth. Although, of course," he added hastily, "such a donation would have no impact on this government's determination to clamp down on tax avoidance. And we will collect the full amount tax that is due – obviously subject to such collection being practical."

"And I wonder about the composition of such a committee," continued Mycroft smoothly. "While, obviously, experts in the field of business and finance will be required, people of a more commonplace background would also require consideration for membership. Would you, Dr Watson, feel you have time to take up such a position? It is hard to think of anyone of my circle of acquaintances who better matches the description I have given."

I was uncertain of what to make of such an unexpected offer.

"I am not sure I am qualified to sit on such a committee," I stammered in the end.

"You would obviously need some instruction," purred Mycroft, "and I am sure the Chancellor would have it in his power to advance you some money on the understanding that you use it to educate yourself so that you can usefully sit on the committee I have proposed."

It took a while for the money to come through, but the letter of guarantee I received of an incoming advance was sufficient for me to obtain a loan securitised (the events of the previous few weeks had certainly taught me a few new financial terms) against my future earnings as a member of the Corporate Remuneration Committee. With this loan I was able to meet the cost of my ill-advised speculation in Hammerson's stock.

Soon my financial troubles were behind me as the membership of the Corporate Remuneration Committee opened the doors to membership of other such committees and to other business opportunities as well.

For reasons that will be obvious, I was unable ever to revert to Mr Holder with advice on whether to make an advance to Mr Beddows.

Afterword by Henry Durham

One of the things one learns by trawling through history is that everything repeats itself.

In 2012, *The Times* newspaper published a report into people taking advantage of a scheme of the type which Mr Beddows makes use of above whereby individuals waived their salary. This gave them access to cash but because the loan was not classed as income they did not have to pay any tax. One of the users of the scheme was the comedian Jimmy Carr who was unapologetic about it until he started being challenged from his audience about it at his stand-up shows. After such challenges caused regular interruptions to his performances, he apologised for "a terrible error of judgment," and said he would stop using it.

Legislation was subsequently enacted to make such schemes more difficult to use, but governments around the world face a constant battle to make sure that tax legislation keeps up with the ingenuity of tax accountants, and it is rare indeed for a national government to be blessed with someone with the talent and insight of a Mycroft Holmes.

The problem was further illustrated as this work was going to press in the summer of 2023 as nine partners at the Australian arm of accountancy firm, PriceWaterhouseCoopers, (which has no connection with Rice, Waterman, Tupper), were suspended for leaking details of Australian government plans to clamp down on tax avoidance to the firm's corporate clients.

EPISODE II

A Modern Odysseus

by Mycroft Holmes

No.

The title does not refer to me or even to my brother, Sherlock, although many might regard our activities as having similarities with the ancient Greek hero, as we single-mindedly use our wiles to solve some of the world's most intractable problems.

The matter that follows identifies a different candidate for the title, and it is only fair to warn readers of a sensitive disposition that the narrative contains features which some may find repugnant.

For my part, I would point out that the events I describe actually happened, and I see no reason why my reader should be shielded from them, just as Dr Watson's accounts of my brother's work did not shield readers from references to a man having his thumb severed with an axe, to another man being the subject of a life-changing vitriol attack, and to Sherlock administering a lethal dose of poison to a stray dog. Some may question the presence of what I am to relate in what is meant to be a textbook on statecraft,

43

but the resolution here, unsatisfactory as some will find it, demonstrates why statecraft sometimes actually prefers an incomplete resolution to its periodic crises.

And what do I mean by an incomplete resolution?

In *The Red-Headed League*, *Black Peter*, and *The Dancing Men*, the initial problem is fully resolved. This is something of a rarity in Dr Watson's chronicles of my brother's activities, for these particular works start with a mystery and end with the criminal being taken into police custody.

By contrast, in many other accounts of my brother's work, the criminal – John Straker in *Silver Blaze* or Jack Stapleton in *The Hound of the Baskervilles* – is dead before he can be apprehended, while in the case of Mr Stark in *The Engineer's Thumb*, or of Rachel Howells in *The Musgrave Ritual*, the malefactor gets clean away.

In other cases, the reason why the legal process does not take its course is that my brother takes it upon himself to act not only as investigator but also as judge. He lets Jack Ryder of *The Blue Carbuncle*, and Charles McCarthy of the *Boscombe Valley Mystery* go free. Jack Ryder is allowed to escape the consequences of his theft because it is Christmas-time – my brother comments in terms grandiloquent even for him, that he may be saving a soul by so doing. And Charles McCarthy, an Australian highwayman, is allowed to die in his bed, so that his daughter may marry the son of one of the men McCarthy murdered without either bride or groom knowing the full facts about the groom's father's death.

I confess I find my brother's judgments rather questionable here and in other similar cases.

I hear of young Sherlock everywhere and I have often wondered why his failure to apprehend more criminals and the judgment he exercises when he does so have not attracted more comment. Maybe on the first matter it is because no one else would have got even as far as my brother, in his own somewhat limited way, was able to do in identifying criminals. And maybe on the second matter, people find his acts of judgment less questionable than I do.

And how might I have done by comparison?

I was subsumed into the service of this country's government at an early age and so the opportunity to work as a detective never arose. And – for here I must be blunt – I do not have the untrammelled energy that youth bestowed on my brother. Despite the manifold shortcomings in his writing, the good Dr Watson had a talent for description. In 1895 he called me heavily built and massive with a suggestion of uncouth physical inertia. I do not disagree with this description however unflattering it may be, but it does mean that, unlike my brother, I cannot undertake to transfix the carcass of a pig with a harpoon as it dangles from a gibbet – another image that will not have been to everyone's taste – or so to box so that my opponent has to be taken home in a cart.

So what can I offer in the place of what I regard as being my brother's somewhat vulgar physicality? My brother has suggested that my specialism is omniscience and there are worse starting points for an investigator than that although this case taught me several things I did not previously know. And my reader will discover, partly for reasons beyond anyone's control, it left as many questions unresolved and as many resolutions as questionable as even the most unresolved and most questionable of my brother's many unresolved and questionable cases. I shall be surprised indeed if everyone agrees with the judgments made in the matter that follows.

It was for the morning of Thursday the 25th of June 1914 that the then Prime Minister, Mr Herbert Asquith, convened a three-day conference of his cabinet and senior civil servants.

I think the conference might have been scheduled for an even more otiose length than the three days allotted to it, but the Prime Minister had a diary date for a Downing Street garden-party for lunchtime on the 28th of June. This was an annual event given in honour of those who were due to be knighted by the King the next day.

As the Prime Minister's Permanent Special Advisor, I had no choice but to attend the conference with its subject, "The role of Government in a time of peace." If I had not attended, I would have had no idea of what reforms might be proposed and how they might be opposed. And, as the party in the garden of Downing Street on the 28th of June was one of the highlights of the London diplomatic calendar, I had no choice but to attend that as well as otherwise there was no knowing what the Prime Minister might agree with the foreign dignitaries there assembled.

In later years a conference of the type described would have been held at Chequers, but that country house was not yet assigned for the use of the Prime Minister, and instead the conference took place at, Wyrley Hall, another location in Buckinghamshire's beautiful Chilterns to the west of London. Much to my irritation, attendees had no choice but to overnight outside London, and even at the early stages of the rather vacuous proceedings, I yearned for the soothing atmosphere of my flat in Pall Mall and the nearby Diogenes Club. I am an early riser, and on the second morning I was out of my bed at five to take a constitutional walk around Wyrley Hall's famous grounds.

Lord Wyrley is not the vulgar type of nobleman who claims to be able to trace his descent to the Normans. On the contrary, Sir Hugo de Ourlli from the Calvados region of Normandy was already on the estate in 1066, and sent a welcoming party to Sussex to greet the man who become known as William the Conqueror on his arrival on these shores. The Wyrley family's great wealth and influence can be traced back to the prudent decision of the present lord's eleventh-century ancestor to side with the Norman duke. The present Lord Wyrley has made the estate his personal plaything and it contains all manner of things features reflecting both the requirements of a wealthy estate owner and his own personal passions: a large staff, extensive stables with a smithy, a cricket-ground, a putting green, a knot garden, an enclosure for His Lordship's hounds, a shooting range, a maze, and a small zoo with animals as diverse as ostriches, kangaroos, and bears. It is no wonder that the estate is often used for gatherings for the panjandrums of government and business.

I perused several of these features during my leisurely wanderings before the sound of furious barking smote my ears. Wondering what was afoot – I thought perhaps a fox or a squirrel was in the area or, worse, had imprudently leapt into the dogs' enclosure – I went to where they are housed.

This is a wire cage, but it has no roof, and a very agile man or beast could climb into it. I could form no conclusion other than that there had indeed been an intruder in the cage as when I got there, even when safely outside the enclosure, I could see that one of the dogs had been attacked with a knife for it had multiple stab wounds, and the beast was howling in its agony.

A young member of the garden staff – also up early – had like me been attracted by the commotion and I asked him to summon the master of hounds. Mr Craddock soon appeared and seemed to know what to do although he looked as shocked by what he saw as I was. He disappeared for a few minutes. When he returned it was on a small carriage and accompanied by his deputy, the lean Mr Curry. They brought with them a stretcher, and a large plaid.

Together the pair went into the cage, laid food out to distract the other dogs, lifted the victim of the attack onto the plaid, and then onto the stretcher, and removed him from the enclosure.

"We are taking Bundo to the vet in Wyrley-St-James," Craddock told me.

"I will come with you," I said, I confess looking for any excuse not to have to be at the conference that day. "This looks like a police matter, and you may need me to make a statement."

I am not sure Craddock was expecting this, but he raised no objection and in a few minutes Craddock, Curry, and I were at the practice of the vet, Mr Allison. The latter, also horrified at the attack, expressed the hope that Bundo could be sedated and stitched. But, alas, the loss of blood had been too great, and, despite the vet's best efforts, Bundo breathed his last as he lay on the treatment table.

Allison was just making the necessary arrangements for the disposal of the body when we heard a commotion coming from the reception area. The four of us – Craddock, Curry, Allison, and I – went out to find a lass of about fifteen in the greatest distress. "I have found a dog dead and pouring blood," she gasped out.

"Where is it?" Allison asked.

"Up Dragon Alley," said she. "I know it's old Mrs Baker's dog, but she can't look after it, so it normally runs almost wild. "Ran," she corrected herself after a second.

Allison agreed to come and have a look and off the four of us and the girl went.

"This is something I have never seen before," said Allison a few minutes later as we stood over the body of the dog that had obviously suffered a horrific death. "Look," he pointed, "someone has not only stabbed the dog – an act horrendous in itself – but they have cut it right open."

He stooped and had a closer look. "They have tried to take out the organs."

"Have they succeeded?" asked Craddock.

Allison examined the dog again.

"The animal has been disembowelled and its heart, liver, and kidney have been ripped out."

"Why would anyone do that?" asked Curry.

"I am a vet, not a medical doctor or a detective. Whoever did this probably belongs to a lunatic asylum rather than to a prison."

"Plenty of lunatics around here," grunted Curry.

For the first time I started to understand the appeal of detective puzzles to my brother.

"What do you mean by that?" I asked.

"I think Mr Curry is referring to Capel Manor which is about two miles outside the town," Craddock replied. "It is a secure establishment for the sick and troubled. It was built about five years ago much to the opposition of local residents. But I have never heard of it having any security problems."

"It only takes one," ground out Curry.

"And has whoever did this actually taken the organs away?" I asked Allison.

"Yes."

I looked at the ground and then all around us. In our rush we had taken no pains to prevent unnecessary footsteps at the site which was an alleyway behind a tavern. Allison saw what I was doing. "It is only half-past-nine, and this was done at least two hours ago judging by the congealing of the blood," said he. "Whoever was responsible, chose a time when they could reckon on being undisturbed. No one will come down an alley behind a pub early in the morning. What were you doing here?" he asked, turning to the girl. "Why, aren't you Violet Harper, the doctor's daughter?" he added.

"Please don't tell my mother," replied the girl, blushing to the roots of her hair, and looking slightly evasive. "I meet one of the lads from the Hall here in the morning before I go to school. We can be undisturbed here. And I am sure my parents wouldn't approve of him."

"This is a matter for the police," said Allison, turning to me.

The police-station was round the corner.

"That was quick, Mr Allison," said the desk-sergeant. "I sent a messenger to your practice asking you to come round here urgently but a couple of minutes ago."

"You sent a message asking for me to come round here? What do you mean?" ejaculated Allison.

"Two stray dogs have been found in different parts of the town. They had both been..."

"Stabbed to death and their organs plucked out?" finished Allison.

"I hadn't told the messenger the details. How do you know?"

"We have just come from Dragon Alley where we found another dog in the same state."

"And we had another case of this up at the Hall," added Craddock and with Allison gave the sergeant a brief account of the two previous cases.

This time accompanied by two officers, Allison and I set off to look at the sites of the two new attacks. Our visits told us nothing new although the scenes were as shocking as they had been at the Wyrley Estate dog enclosure and at Dragon Alley. One of the attacks had taken place in Pullman's Yard and the other in Friar's Place, both little visited cul-de-sacs turning off major roads.

"Whoever did this, knew that here too he was likely to remain undisturbed," said Allison grimly as we stood at Friar's Place.

"So, what could be the motive behind this?" I asked. "A lunatic might kill dogs, but why would he strip them of their organs?"

"Beats me, sir," said one of the constables, "I've never seen anything like it. If we really have a lunatic on the loose – and I have no information that one has escaped – there is no limit to what he might do or where he might stop. It might be humans next."

"That's why I opposed the building of Capel Manor," grunted Curry grimly. "It's in my village and it's a blight on us all."

There was not much more to say, and Craddock, Curry, and I returned to Wyrley Hall where the attacks were the sole topic of discussion.

The next morning, I was not surprised when the police in the shape of the slim Inspector MacDermott, originally from Dublin, arrived to conduct the official investigation. As I had been the person who had discovered the attack on the dog, I was the first person to be interviewed, and we went to the dog enclosure together. I explained to MacDermott why I was at Wyrley Hall and how I had come to be at the cage. He looked me up and down and said with a ghost of smile, "Well, even though I suspect you have no alibi for a walk at half past five in the morning, I think your figure rules out the possibility of you having climbed over the wire into the cage."

"My younger brother's skill in promoting his largely meretricious talent for deductive reasoning has obviously had its impact on you. But to your point, only an agile person would be able to climb over the wire mesh to get into the cage unless they had a key to the padlock and, as you remark, I am of a large frame and have no access to a key."

When I explained who my brother was, a look of wonder came over MacDermott's face.

"I have no clues on this matter which the whole county will be up in arms about. It would be an honour to work with you, Mr Holmes, if you would be prepared to join me on the investigation. And indeed, if the public knew that a Mr Holmes was here and I had not asked him for help, I think I know what the reaction would be."

Despite my lack of experience of detective work, the prospect of another day listening to politicians expatiate on government appalled me. Their specialism is self-publicity and mine is what my reader is reading about in this work. Thus, the simple answer to all their problems is to leave the running of the country to me while they concentrate their energies on seeking re-election by recommending to the electorate whatever I enact. Accordingly, I was happy to accede to MacDermott's request. In the text that follows my readers will understand that I cannot show representations of any of the people who were the subject of the investigation.

"Let us," I suggested, "start by speaking to Mr Craddock and then to Lord Wyrley."

Craddock was unable to add much to the picture. "I have worked with hounds and dogs for thirty years," said he, "and I have never seen anything like this. I was just getting up when Samson, one of the junior gardening hands, on his way to the early shift, banged on my door and told me about what you had discovered, Mr Holmes."

"So, you have quarters on the estate?"

"Yes, the senior staff – so Lord Wyrley's secretary, the butler, the head-chef, the chief-groom, the zoo-keeper, His Lordship's valet, and the chief lady-in-waiting – all have houses near the great hall. Most of the rest of the staff, like Mr Curry, live off-site, and come and go in shifts."

"Have there been any more untoward events on the estate?" I asked.

"Well," said Craddock after a moment's hesitation, "I would have said not, but Mr Droy, the zoo-keeper, told me this morning that he thought someone had been trying to get into the bear-cage. You'll have to talk to him about the details. But he told me that whoever had tried to get in, had not got anywhere. I will have to improve security for our dogs after this."

Droy was summoned, "Someone had tried to saw through the padlock," he confirmed. "There's a thick metal bolt so you either have to break the padlock or the bolt. There was a little of pile of iron filings on the ground when I went to the cage yesterday, but you'd need time, strength, and a big saw to get through a bolt like that. And goodness knows what our bears would have done if the intruder had got in."

"Had you reported it to anyone?"

"I had mentioned it to Mr Craddock but that was before the attack on the dogs. I am not at all sure what is the point of reporting an attempt to get into the bear-cage to anyone else where the perpetrator so obviously did not know what he was doing and had been so unsuccessful in it. But I did put a second padlock on the bolt."

"Do you have any ideas about the tool used?"

"It must have been a file or a small hack-saw."

"Where might one get hold of such a tool on this estate?"

"I go to the blacksmith when I need a tool of any sort."

"But there are not many other people who would have a credible reason to go the smithy to seek a file, unless the tool was stolen."

"That may be so, but I beg you won't try to drag me into the matter, Mr Holmes. There have been attacks not just here but also at Wyrley-St-James and I am sure you are better off seeking a solution there."

"We had better speak to Lord Wyrley about what he knows about his staff," said MacDermott to me when Droy had gone. "We can use the drawing room to interview people, as the library is being used for the conference."

His Lordship came and brought his secretary with him. Lord Wyrley was a tall, bearded man of about sixty whose slightly bow-legged gait bore witness to a love of the chase. His secretary, Edalji, by contrast, was a slight man of apparently Indian extraction, and in his mid-thirties.

"Could you keep this brief?" requested Wyrley in the absent voice of someone whose interests are far away as soon as personal introductions of had been gone through.

"I will make every endeavour to do so, your lordship," said MacDermott respectfully.

"With the Prime Minister and the Cabinet to attend to here," continued Wyrley almost before MacDermott had finished speaking, "I have got some rather more important matters to deal with than attacks on dogs. And, obviously," he added with a complacent wave of the hand, "I and my family won't have had anything to do with attacks on dogs, although I assume you'll want to exclude my staff from your enquiries."

"I would not associate someone with your background with matters such as these, Lord Wyrley," said MacDermott although Lord Wyrley had already risen to leave and was halfway out of the door by the time MacDermott had said it. After a pause,

Wyrley's secretary, who had not said anything, dutifully followed his master, and MacDermott made no attempt to stop him.

MacDermott turned to me. "It must be the mere presence of a Mr Holmes here," he said, looking rather pleased with himself, "that I am on such good form. I inferred that your bulk meant you could not be responsible for the attack in the dog-pen, and that their social class excluded His Lordship and his family from the investigation."

"And you did not want to interview his secretary?"

"Knowledge of Indian customs meant that I could conclude that His Lordship's secretary could not have had anything to do with it either."

"Why not?"

"As a Hindu, he would have been afraid to attack an animal. It might have been one of his reincarnated relatives. They teach us policeman a lot about cultural matters these days and it helps us in deductive reasoning. And it helps to make up for the lack of resources they give us. I've got to investigate this case on my own – there's no money to give me anyone else – and it's just as well I was able to involve y..."

A thought suddenly struck him.

"As I have excluded Edalji from the enquiry, I can use him as a note taker. That will make my life a lot easier. As he's Lord Wyrley's secretary, I assume his English is up to it."

"But how will the other staff react to a colleague being involved in your questioning?"

"You make a good point," said MacDermott thoughtfully. "But there's a large cupboard in that corner over there and Edalji can take his place in it. Indians are used to... well, I would not want to say anything that would betray any sort of prejudice on my part."

Edalji was summoned and he was eager to serve.

"It would be an honour to be the amanuensis of a case conducted by Mr Holmes even if it is not the great Mr Sherlock Holmes," he said when he heard who I was.

"It will be I who will be conducting the case," said MacDermott in a slightly prickly voice, "and I will need the approval of Lord Wyrley before I can presume to engage you, Mr Edalji."

But once MacDermott had obtained Wyrley's approval, Edalji seated himself cross-legged on the floor of the cupboard with a note-pad on his knee.

The first person to be questioned was Summers, the butler whose grey hair was combed over his pate from just above his left ear.

"I was here on site throughout but have not been out of the house for two days," said he, in a gravelly tone, his eyes fixed straight ahead. "I could not therefore be associated with the attacks either here or in Wyrley-St-James."

"What were you doing?"

"I was attending to my duties and to my own personal matters when not on duty."

"Is there anything specific you would like to draw our attention to?"

"I fear I have my hands full enough without spending my time looking out for people who want to attack dogs."

And with that Summers was on his way.

"Summers's situation certainly means he has his hands full," came Edalji's voice from the cupboard.

"What do you mean?"

"He threw over his wife two years ago, but she remains on the estate staff as Lady Wyrley's dresser. Their paths must cross frequently. He has since taken up with a much younger member of the kitchen staff, Miss Beryl Gillies."

"What of that?"

"Summers has confided in me," said Edalji, a note of pride in his voice.

"What has he confided in you?"

"'I find it hard to keep up with such a demanding woman,'" quoted Edalji in a voice uncommonly like Summers but with a tone on the cusp of panic. "I remember," Edalji continued, "that Summers was mopping his brow as he said that. 'I really don't know what there is that I can do about it,' is another of his favourite sayings."

"What sort of demands does she make?"

"He did not specify. But it was the talk of those of us who live under the stairs that he had started receiving packages from Prague which he took unopened to his own quarters. And the speculation became only more lurid about what was in these packages when Dr Watson published *The Crooked Man* about a rejuvenating serum derived from monkeys made by a Mr Lowenstein of Prague."

"I see," replied MacDermott.

"Shall I add that to the record?" asked Edalji from his cupboard.

"Please do so."

The next interviewee was with the head cook, Monsieur Robert Le Fèvre, a tall Frenchman in his mid- thirties. Although he spoke English, it was the English of a Frenchman which I try to reproduce below.

"I attended to my *cuisine* – duties in the kitchen. And I also have my wife to deal with," he replied when asked about his movements.

"You have your wife to deal with?"

"She is consumptive. Her death is, *hélas*, it is only a matter of time. When I am not working in the kitchen, I am tending to her."

"What is a Frenchman doing here in the Chilterns?"

Le Fèvre gave a Gallic shrug.

"It is hardly unusual for a Frenchman to use his skills with food to travel the world. I cook here for the English aristocracy and its politicians, I have worked in schools in Switzerland and Germany, and I have accompanied exploration missions to Africa, the Himalayas, and the Polar regions. It is the same discipline no matter what I do. Making the best use of limited resources."

Le Fèvre exited and Edalji piped up.

"Our chef omitted to mention that he seeks solace in the arms of some of the more junior of the kitchen staff. Florence Blount, the scullery maid, is his preferred choice of company at present. I see them together sometimes. Edalji's voice suddenly acquired a French accent as he said, "Florence! Florence!" in an animated fashion with an unmistakable French emphasis on the second syllable of the word and a rolled R. Edalji's voice then went up an octave as he said "Robert! Robert!" in an equally emotional tone but this time rendered with a Buckinghamshire burr.

"I see."

"Do you want me add that to the record as well?"

"Please do so."

Next came Stringer, the head-groom, a tall thin man with a mournful expression.

"I am an early riser and only come into the Hall to sleep as I spend the rest of my time with the horses."

"So where were you early yesterday morning?"

"I spent the night in the stables as a mare was foaling."

"So, you were up all night?"

"Indeed so, but fully occupied. And we have a new foal to show for my endeavours. And no need to call the vet."

"But no witnesses."

"No human ones."

Again, Edalji's voice from the cupboard provided more information after our interviewee had departed.

"Mr Stringer is a recent addition to the staff. He is harsher to his equine charges than anyone else I have seen. Lord Wyrley has already observed that he does not envy that new-born foal when it gets broken in by Mr Stringer. Stringer himself says – and here Edalji again put skill for mimicry on display such that it was as if Stringer were back in the room with us as we heard a gloomy voice intone – 'I will do whatever is necessary to get the best out of my horses. Animals do not respect you unless they know that you have a little bit of devil.'"

Edalji's pithy character sketches of the Wyrley Hall staff meant that we learnt far more about the staff from his candid opinions than we learnt from MacDermott's unrevealing line of questioning. I spoke to Edalji over lunch.

"There cannot be many people of Indian extraction in a position like yours."

"I had not really given the matter any thought. I was born in this country as was my mother and I have never been to India. My father is a Parsee who has become a country parson in Staffordshire, so I do not regard myself as Indian at all. I do not cleave to the same beliefs about animals that many Indians do. I eat the same diet as most people with both parents born in this country do. Outside my duties for Lord Wyrley, my chief passion is cricket which is a sport invented by the English and working for an employer who has his own cricket ground allows me to pursue it. With my small stature and natural agility, I am well suited to the role of keeping wicket for the Wyrley Estate team. My time spent squatting low behind the stumps was good practice for sitting in the cupboard this morning."

The conference adjourned on the afternoon of Saturday the 27th of June, and I returned to London with the intent of returning to

Wyrley the next week to work with MacDermott should my commitments allow.

So it was that I was in my flat in Pall Mall on the morning of the 28th of June. I was standing before the glass to make sure my dress was in order for the garden-party when there was a knock at the door and the boy in buttons announced, "Mr Sherlock Holmes to see you."

I had not seen Sherlock for some time. I knew, of course, that he had been active in espionage, but I did not know he had seen fit to grow a rather ragged goatee.

"These are the sacrifices one makes for one's country, good brother," said Sherlock, pulling at the little tuft on his chin, "but there is another matter I have been investigating that I would wish to draw to your attention."

"I am at your disposal although I would advise you that my attendance is shortly required at a garden party in Downing Street for those being knighted tomorrow."

"It is that I would wish to speak to you about."

"Pray continue," said I.

"Among those being knighted is the Australian explorer, Douglas Mawson."

Most of those who receive a knighthood in this country are politicians who have had to stand down due to incompetence or corruption or both and demand a knighthood as their price for their silence on topics embarrassing for the Prime Minister. The recently knighted Sir William Gavinson is an example of this category. Others are long-serving civil-servants who claim (with no tangible foundation) that they could earn more if they worked in the City of London, and regard a knighthood as recompense for a princely salary foregone. Sir Montague Proud or Montague Proud as he was on the morning of the 28th of June 1914 was a prime case of this. If the politicians are being paid with a knighthood for not saying what they might, then civil servants are being knighted for doing what they are paid to do.

I was aware that Mawson amongst other luminaries had been nominated for a knighthood for his adventuring in Antarctica although I confess I could see no reason why a man should be singled out for having, as far as I could make out, done no more than confirming that the polar regions are indeed cold, snowy, and inhospitable. As I recalled, he had been on an expedition with two companions establishing this point but had returned to his base-camp on his own.

"It's like this," confirmed my brother when I expressed the above to him. "Mawson's mission took him into the Antarctic wastes with two companions, Belgrave Ninnis, an Englishman; and Dr Xavier Mertz, a Swiss. Ninnis fell into a crevasse along with most of the party's food and six of their dogs. They were not seen again. Mertz and Mawson made to return to base camp but weakened as their remaining stock of food ran out. To survive, they shot and ate their sledge-dogs, but Mertz got weaker and weaker. Eventually he was only strong enough be able to ingest the offals of the huskies as opposed to their tough flesh. He finally expired two hundred miles from base camp. Mawson made the rest of the journey back on his own."

The outlines of the events my brother described were known to me, but the details had passed me by, and I remained unclear what it was in them that he wanted to talk to me about.

"During my absence after the events of the Reichenbach Falls, I undertook some explorations of my own presenting myself as a Norwegian called Sigersen. Hearing of my exploits, I was asked by the British Institute of Explorers to investigate what might be learnt from Mawson's disasters."

"I see."

"One of my findings was that dog's liver is known in explorer circles as being poisonous to humans as this was not the first time that explorers had used the expedient of eating normal food on the outward part of the journey and living off their pack animals on the return. So, you may be about to attend a garden-party being held in honour of a man who fed his companion poison in order to survive himself, and who is to be knighted tomorrow."

Extraordinary though these revelations were, there seemed nothing much else to discuss with my brother, but I did have one other question.

"Did your investigation identify any other animals whose organs are poisonous to humans?"

"Now that you mention it," said my brother looking surprised at my question, "I did discover that bear's liver is also poisonous to humans. But that was not relevant to Mawson's explorations in Antarctica as a bear is not a pack animal and there are no wild animals in the frozen wastes of that continent which a desperate human might seek to consume."

I gave a low chuckle, and said, "A long shot, dear brother, a very long shot."

My response, as had been my intention, seemed rather to disconcert young Sherlock, but there was nothing further to discuss, and he was soon on his way. His departure enabled me to give the matter he had raised due consideration.

The other people being knighted were, as I have indicated, in most cases being honoured for not doing what they could have done or for doing what they were supposed to do anyway. But they had not done anything which would be regarded as beyond the pale if it came into the public domain. Here was a man who had been feted as a hero, who was about to be knighted, and yet his alleged conduct was bound to cause a scandal if it became public knowledge. But equally, withdrawing the offer of a knighthood would only raise questions among the public to which it might prove impossible to give a definite answer. In the end I decided the matter would have to be put to the Prime Minister and I walked to Downing Street as briskly as I could to get there before any of the guests arrived.

"He and his companion ate dog's flesh?" exclaimed Asquith when I put to him the accusation of my brother in an anteroom. "And Mawson fed his companion dog's liver which poisoned him?"

"So, my brother Sherlock alleges."

"And he knew the effect that such consumption had on humans?

"My brother was unable to be sure on that point. It is plausible that an experienced polar hand like Mawson would have had knowledge of this although not certain. It will equally be impossible for him or for anyone else to prove that he did not know."

"We must have this matter out with him. We cannot have this man knighted when there are potential accusations of this sort which may arise against him after he has been ennobled. I have every regard for your brother's investigative skills and for his discretion, but this matter is bound to come out at some point."

Douglas Mawson

1882 - 1958

A few minutes later Mawson arrived. He was accompanied by the Australian High Commissioner, Sir George Reid, who expressed his pride on his arrival at the ennobling of his compatriot. The picture of Mawson on the left-hand side of the page renders description of the explorer superfluous but the intensity of expression he bore that day is well captured by it.

Asquith had arranged for a discrete request be made to Mawson to join Asquith and me in a small ante room of Downing Street. As a decision to cancel the award of a knighthood would have implications for Anglo-Australian relations, it was agreed that Reid should be present while Asquith and I taxed Mawson with what I hesitate to call my brother's accusation, but I find no other term suffices.

Asquith laid out the gravamen of the charge and concluded with the remark, "You appreciate there can be no chance of awarding a knighthood if these accusations can be substantiated."

Mawson looked straight back at the Prime Minister.

"I swear I had no idea that dog's liver is poisonous to humans."

"The tell us about what happened."

"After Ninnis had disappeared into the crevasse with most of our provisions, Mertz and I were three-hundred miles from base with no hope of rescue and only enough food for two men for a week.

66

We had no choice but to eat the dogs. We would eat a few ounces each day of the ordinary food and mix the two together."

"And?"

"As we made our way across the wasteland, Mertz seemed to lose the will to move and wished only to remain in his sleeping bag. He began to deteriorate rapidly and had violent fits. At one point he bit off the tip of his own little finger. Dog meat is almost fatless and tough to chew so I gave Mertz more of the softer offals as he found those easier to ingest. He died on the 8th of January 1913. I did the final two-hundred miles on my own. If I had known liver was poisonous, we would have left it uneaten, but I had no knowledge of this and indeed, after Mertz died, I ate it myself."

Mawson was asked to leave the room and Asquith, Reid, and I sat in colloquy.

"It seems to me," said Asquith who had been a successful barrister before going into politics, "that we are in realms where the normal laws no longer apply. Mawson has denied any knowledge vehemently, but let us assume that he did indeed know that dog's liver is poisonous to humans. Are we to criticise him for the way he behaved in a situation where the survival of one of the two adventurers may require the death of the other?"

"Are we to reward such behaviour with a knighthood?" I asked.

Reid, had also originally been a barrister, and countered, "Mawson has been hailed a hero in my country for his survival against all odds. It has been described as the greatest survival story in history. After Mertz died, Mawson himself fell into a crevasse and survived only because the sledge to which he was harnessed lodged in the crevasse aperture and he was able to climb up the harness."

"Odysseus," mused Asquith who had studied Classics with great distinction before he had become a barrister, "is regarded as one of the greatest heroes of all time. Yet he returned to his home island of Ithaca after ten years soldiering and seven years in the arms of the nymph Calypso not only with no plunder from the Trojan War but having lost the entire army of soldiers and the fleet of ships with which he set out. And Mawson's achievements amount to mapping a wasteland."

"And yet Odysseus's throne was restored to him on his return," countered Reid. "Australia is a young country, and we need heroes of our own."

"I pity the country that has a need for heroes."

Although in the presence of two barristers, I felt it fell to me to summarise the arguments. "The knighthood for Mawson is being given for surviving an extreme ordeal. Surely that is all that anyone would seek to do. Are the features of this ordeal so extraordinary, that they merit this special recognition? Or do we have any hard evidence Mawson knew of the toxicity of what he fed his companion?"

"I think not," broke in Reid. "I heard sincerity in his voice when he denied it and saw it in his gaze too. And he said he ate the same as his companion so there is no evidence that the toxic viands were the only cause of Mertz's death. It will create a huge row if the investiture is now cancelled. And it will require an investigation of his behaviour which, if it is to condemn it, will need to prove he acted deliberately to poison his comrade and for which he will be the sole witness. And his explorations took him to places previously untrodden by man and his return from them, whatever the circumstances, shows an indomitable spirit."

"Heroism and its recognition require the hero to have had a choice between doing the right thing and the wrong thing. Mawson chose to go on his adventure, but his survival was not an exercise of choice. The only choice he may have exercised was one that may have resulted in the death of his companion."

"'May'. You have used the word twice. 'May'," objected Reid. The word was still hanging in the air as there came a hurried tap on the door. A look of annoyance crossed Asquith's face, but it opened before he could ask for us to be left undisturbed.

It was the Foreign Secretary, Mr Edward Grey, another obligatory attendee at such a garden-party.

"Gentlemen," he said in a voice of the great gravity, "I just have received a telegram that the heir to the Austro-Hungarian crown, Prince Franz Ferdinand, was assassinated in Sarajevo this morning. The Austrians have already blamed the Serbians and are threatening them with invasion. I have just come from the Foreign Office which is buzzing like an upturned beehive. There is no knowing what will happen next."

"If the Austrians respond by launching an attack on the Serbs, the Germans will join the Austrians," I surmised. "The Russians will then come to the aid of the Serbs, and the French will mobilise against the Germans. Great Britain will hold the balance of power in Europe. If the Germans choose to attack the French through Belgium – and they were within five miles of the Belgian border when they beat the French at Sedan in their 1871 invasion – this country is bound by the 1839 Treaty of London to go the Belgians' rescue."

"This country and its Empire of which Australia is a key part," intoned Reid, I suspect to the bafflement of Grey who was not aware of the previous exchanges.

All eyes turned to Asquith, but he deferred to me.

"If we pull Mawson's investiture now, the process used to make the award will be called into question. And it will cause huge controversy across the Empire. We have no hard evidence of wrong-doing, only suspicions which have been denied, and no investigation will be able to disprove the denials," I summarised.

There was a long silence before Asquith finally made his decision.

"I will have to let it go ahead," he said at last. "I may have more important matters to address in the very near future. Or the whole thing may blow over. Let us adjourn to the garden."

My reader will hardly have failed to have noted the links between the Mawson matter and events at Wyrley Hall. While at Wyrley the killings and dismemberments had seemed motiveless when MacDermott and I had investigated them, now the harvesting of canine organs for use as a poison provided a clear motive for them. And yet I could dedicate no time to pursue the matter for, as guests stated to arrive, it became clear that word of the assassination in Sarajevo was spreading through London's diplomats like wildfire. As I moved from conversation group to conversation group I heard exchanges like, "Would Britain really go to war for a scrap of paper signed three quarters a century ago?", "How many divisions could France field in three weeks?", "Will the Germans capture Paris again like they did in 1871?" and "Where is the British Navy?"

The first three questions were all a matter of speculation and opinions varied. But the last question was one of fact which I was in a position to answer. On the 28th of June 1914 the British Navy was at Kiel, the German Navy's main harbour, on a long pre-arranged goodwill visit.

When I finally got back to my quarters in Pall Mall it was to find a messenger had left a despatch from Inspector MacDermott which ran as follows:

28 June, 1914

Dear Mr Holmes,

You asked me to keep you updated about the progress of our investigation at Wyrley.

The work at Wyrley Hall which you and I carried out yesterday conducted found no motive for the attacks and no suspect, and I was originally due to carry out further work at the Hall tomorrow, Monday the 29th of June. But at lunchtime I got word that the wife of Mr Le Fèvre, the head-cook, had died in her sleep, and so I would have switched the focus of my investigation to the town of Wyrley-St-James.

But the matter may have resolved itself this afternoon, for, when the Sunday papers carrying reports of the outrages were published, one of the inmates of Capel Manor made a full though vague confession.

Royden Sharp is of gentle birth but had been detained after previous attacks on wild animals, the nature of which I will spare you. If these earlier outrages had been against farm stock, a criminal offence would have been committed justifying a custodial sentence. As these outrages were carried out on wild animals, no criminal offence had taken place, so detention in a secure establishment was the only measure available.

Sharp claims to have been able to fool guards at the main entrance to get out of Capel Manor in the evening and to get back in again the following day. Security will now be tightened at Capel Manor.

While there must remain doubts about this explanation of the attacks, as long as no further attacks occur, it will prove to have been the right one. I will of course update you if anything further untoward takes place.

I would like to place on record my thanks for your assistance in this matter and remain,

Yours truly,

Patrick MacDermott

As my reader will understand, late June 1914 was a point when the world was about to go mad as threats gave way to mobilisations and thence to war.

But in my small corner of Pall Mall, I had an explanation for a mystery as my brother's accusations about Mawson gave a reason for the killing and evisceration of the dogs at Great Wyrley, a clear suspect as the perpetrator of the attacks, and a human victim. While the explanation MacDermott had for the outrages in Wyrley might indeed be the correct one, it would be astonishing if Le Fèvre, with his background in exploration and food-provision, had not had knowledge of the toxicity of what was being harvested. And he had both the means to administer a poison and, with his ailing wife and a young sweetheart, a motive to do so. Whether an investigation of him would have been able to prove any of this, is, of course, an open question.

And yet Royden Sharp's confession meant there was no need for an investigation which, even if it had been inconclusive on events at Wyrley, could hardly have failed to have linked events there with Mawson whose image it is planned to put onto Australian notes and coins, and whose name will be attached to buildings and mountains across Australia. The whole concept of public honours would have been called into question at a time when the state needed to draw on its citizens' goodwill for the sacrifices required by the greatest war the world has seen.

As it was, there were no further outrages at Wyrley and public interest in the matter faded as the outbreak of the Great War drove all other matters from public consciousness.

The passage of time has made it by no means clearer who was responsible for the Wyrley attacks. There is no evidence that Sharp ever left the confines of Capel Manor again and by the end of July 1914, the widowed Le Fèvre had joined up with the French forces. By the end of August 1914, he had been mortally wounded in an attack on a German machine gun post for which he received the posthumous award of the Légion d'honneur. But before he made his way to France, he had already married Florence Blount who was with child, and I cannot help but wonder whether the discovery that his sweetheart was pregnant prompted him to commit what became known as the Wyrley outrages.

So, the investigation at Wyrley came to an end with a solution that satisfied the public even though I was by no means convinced it was the right one. But this published solution stopped any difficult questions being asked about the propriety of the award to Mawson. Thus, all was well and within two months, the British and the Australians were in lockstep as they declared war on Germany and her allies.

Afterword by Henry Durham

The British honours system – knighthoods, baronetcies, noble orders, and the like – are one of the means at the disposal of the British Government to reward behaviour which might not be considered as being for the common good. Prime Ministers Lloyd George in 1922, Harold Wilson in 1976, Tony Blair in 2007, and David Cameron in 2016 were all accused of selling honours in exchange for donations to their parties. Lloyd George had a price list for each rank of honour starting at £10,000 for a knighthood, Wilson gave honours to two men subsequently investigated for fraud, and Blair was interviewed by the police, and it emerged during the investigation of Blair, that everyone who had donated more than £1 million to the Labour Party during his time as leader had been elevated to the House of Lords.

In fact, the largest body of honours go to civil servants for their service which might be considered as part of their job and to politicians for being lobby-fodder for the Government.

EPISODE III

A Goat in the Government

Foreword by Mycroft Holmes

David Lloyd George

1863 - 1945

No British prime minister has been – nor, I trust, in the future will ever be – forced to take arms against such a sea of troubles as that which confronted David Lloyd George in the years 1918 and 1919. A war on a scale unprecedented in living memory raged across continental Europe, and a global plague added millions to the toll of deaths already claimed by that war.

In the events set out below, I learnt that the Prime Minister had a private life which explains the title of the next episode in this collection – for the "goat" of the title refers not to my own status among the greats of all time as a practitioner of statecraft but rather to Mr Lloyd George's priapic proclivities. I also learnt that he had a relationship with the truth that was casual at best. This combination of factors came close to toppling him, yet I was able to fulfil my primary function of ensuring that the ship of state proceeded on its way as serenely as events allowed with no one lost overboard.

The rest of this episode is narrated by Dr Watson and brother, Sherlock, plays a leading role. My sibling shows all his usual investigative skill and zeal along with a lack of strategic acumen which illustrates what Dr Watson meant when he said my brother's understanding of politics was nil.

A Goat in the Government – Dr Watson writes

"So, Miss Pendry," I asked my patient after having listened to her description of her unseasonal chill in May 1918, "do you smoke?"

"Well, Doctor," replied the fair young lady thoughtfully, "I do not. But I am tempted to do so. I am of gentle stock – in more normal times, I would be spending my time looking for a husband – but since the call for women to work, I have been working as a tram-conductress. Most of my fellow workers and my passengers smoke. But I do not – or at least I have not yet started."

"Then I really think it is time you did so," I replied firmly. "A cigarette is an excellent barrier against outside infection, and if I am blunt, the supply situation caused by this war means that the apothecary will have precious little to offer you as a remedy in any case. I smoke 'Ships' tobacco myself, one of the most robust tobaccos one can find, or at least I do whenever it is obtainable, and I have not suffered a day's illness for years."

In the first half of 1918 there was no end in sight to the war to end wars. I still had the medical practice in Queen Square which I had founded on my second marriage in 1907 but the world had become unrecognisable since then.

Places of entertainment had been closed for more than three years, endless parades of what were to my eyes horribly young-looking soldiers marched down nearby Southampton Row, there had been night flights by Zeppelins dropping bombs on London, and the introduction of food-rationing had been announced. And then there were the seemingly endless casualty lists. Deaths routinely ran at fifteen to twenty thousand a month across the country. I could only bring myself to look at the list of casualties from Bloomsbury which were pasted up on boards in Bloomsbury Square as the numbers were easier to grasp. I saw sons of friends and neighbours thickly represented among the fallen. The flower of our youth I thought grimly, relieved that my elder son, Edward, still a mere seven, was too young to be called to arms for a few years at least. I hoped the conflict would be at an end by the time he would be eligible for call-up but there was no sign that this would be the case.

My patient, a woman of twenty-three, who in normal circumstances would have had no difficulty in attracting a queue of suitors, but who might now struggle to find a husband at all, departed. She was followed by a Corporal Billings who was on leave from Flanders. Normally, he told me, he worked as a bookbinder. He also described symptoms of a chill. He was a smoker already and I sent him on his way urging him to smoke more and perhaps a stronger tobacco. I added the comment that unseasonal chills seemed to be doing their worst but that there was probably nothing I could do for him.

After a few more consultations, I had started thinking about my afternoon round of patient visits when there was a commotion in my waiting-room.

"I must see Dr Watson immediately! My daughter is in convulsions!" I heard a panic-stricken voice cry.

I put my head out of the door of my consulting room to see a woman who bore an obvious family resemblance to Miss Pendry.

Mrs Pendry saw me and said, "Dr Watson, my daughter had a fit of fever when she came home from here. She is lying on her bed and keeps going into spasm. You must come at once."

I was down the steps immediately and five minutes at the maximum speed my sixty-six-year-old legs could carry me saw us at Milman Street, a quiet road with houses in yellow-brown brick down both sides. The Pendry's lived in Number 12, and I could hear stentorian gasps in an upstairs room as I entered. Up I went to the source of the sound to find my patient of a mere hour or two previously rendered a wreck of the fine young woman she had been. Her skin had acquired a bluish tinge and I could see a pulse pound furiously at her temple. As I entered, she leant over a bowl and from her mouth exploded clots of bile and blood. When she had finished vomiting, there issued from her nose a torrent of more blood mixed with catarrh.

At length she stopped and sat bolt upright in her bed, eyes glazed, and unable to speak.

Her mother had joined us.

"It started as soon as she came back from seeing you, Doctor. She came in, sat down, and then said she felt very unwell. The vomiting followed almost immediately."

"Where has she been that she could have picked up something like this?"

"You will have heard from her that she works on the trams. It is a most unfitting role for a young lady of her class. And it means she mingles with thousands of the meanest people every day. And it probably won't have done her much good going to your surgery either."

I was not sure whether the last sally was intended as a reproach to my care but saw no point in responding. And beyond issuing instructions that my patient should rest – not that she was going to be able to do anything else – and keep warm, I had nothing to offer for an illness the like of which in its suddenness and intensity I had never seen before, and I was soon back at the practice.

I was in no mood for any more medical work that day and went to the residential part of the house. I had been there no longer than ten minutes when there was a knock at the front-door. Getting hold of good domestic servants is difficult at the best of times and impossible in time of war, so it was I who went to answer it myself. There on the step stood Mycroft Holmes who said, "May I come in, Dr Watson? I need to speak to you in the strictest confidence." He spoke in a manner which did not appear to give me any choice and I took him to my consulting room.

By 1918 Mycroft Holmes was in his early seventies and, with his great corpulence, showed every sign of his age, although his grey eyes retained their piercing gaze. I have remarked elsewhere that Sherlock Holmes is not given to anything that could conceivably be described as small talk, and in my dealings with him in the past, this description had applied even more to my friend's elder brother. It was therefore something of a surprise that when he had sat down Mycroft asked airily, "How is your practice at the present time, good Doctor? Is everything normal given the conditions of war? Or have you seen anything unusual?"

"Being a doctor, one is constantly coming across new things," I replied cautiously.

"Is there any particular reason why you say that?" pressed Mycroft.

In the end I felt impelled to give Mycroft a full account of the consultation I had had with Miss Pendry – I also mentioned the consultation with Corporal Billings – although I withheld any details that might betray the identify of either.

To my surprise, Mycroft's response was to rub his hands together as though in satisfaction.

"I thought as much," he said almost gleefully. "You must keep details of this case and of any similar cases you encounter to yourself, Dr Watson. We must not give our enemy succour by letting him know that there is anything untoward going on in this country. For your information, there have been people struck down by a fever of the type you describe in Italy and Spain, and I dare say that it will eventually become impossible to withhold the fact that we have had outbreaks in this country too. But for the moment, I think we should confine reports to overseas outbreaks."

And saying not another word, Mycroft rose, and made his way out of the house.

As had so often been the case in my dealings with Mycroft Holmes, I was left turning over in my head what his comments might mean. He would not, I thought, have troubled to see me on a small matter and since he had only expressed an interest in the shocking case of Miss Pendry, something of greater significance than a single inexplicable and, I feared, grave incident must be afoot. I resolved to follow the press and see how the outbreak of this new disease was covered in Spain.

The next day I went to the newsagent after and looked at the papers arrayed on the counter.

During these grim times the newspapers were uniformly dominated by what was happening in the war and, as I looked at *The Times, The Telegraph, The Mail,* and *The Herald,* today seemed no different. Usually, I paid no heed to the more popular end of the press, but I noticed that *The Globe,* at this sombre period the closest there was to a light read, carried a quite different story from all the other newspapers.

The Globe had built a reputation for what it called turnover articles.

In such articles, the content of a page was so salacious, the reader felt impelled to turn over to the next page where the article continued, and this description applied precisely to the front page that caught my eye. Under the headline, MYSTERIOUS EVENTS IN MADRID, stood an article which stated under the by-line of what was described as the Globe's special

81

correspondent, Webster Stevenson, "Watchers of the doings of foreign monarchs will have been intrigued by the postponement of the opening of Parliament in neutral Spain due to a sudden illness of King Alfonso XIII. The illness seems to be more than the normal round of influenza that circulates periodically through Madrid and there are rumours of a wider-spread contagion among the population." The article continued in a way that made the mystery more titillating but actually added very little to this first paragraph. It concluded with the comment, "*The Globe's* Spanish correspondent will do all he can to clear up this mystery for its readers."

"Everyone's looking at *The Globe* today," grunted the newsagent, Mr Strother, when he saw what I was looking at. "There's bugs goin' around and no one'll tell us anything about them. I don't know if this is the same thing and Lawd knows where they come from. Probably them Germans spreading 'em."

"Where did you hear about bugs going around?" I asked.

"I 'ears everything that is going on round here. Mr Hussey across the road. He died of it suddenly last night. Came 'ome sick from the brickworks and never lifted his head again. An' Mrs Autumn two houses down from here. Here one day, gorn the next."

I bought a copy of *The Globe* – "Just like everyone else has done today," grumbled Strother. "It shows where we've got to. People would rather read about a killer disease than about a killer war." – and went on my way.

Over the next two weeks there was an extraordinary growth in activity at my practice as more and more patients came to my surgery displaying the same unfathomable symptoms as Miss

Pendry and whom I was as powerless to treat as I had been to treat her.

To try to prevent the spread of the disease, the government introduced stringent measures to restrict the number of social interactions people might have although, at first, the new restrictions were attributed to the exigencies of war.

My reader may imagine how difficult and ultimately futile imposing restrictions on social interactions was when London was a major staging post for troops passing through it on the way to fight in France. Nevertheless, a ban was imposed on gatherings of people from different households – this, even though the idea of holding any sort of major social event at a time like this was absurd. The few businesses which could be plausibly described as non-essential to the war-effort and that were still open were ordered to close. Schools were also ordered to shut which created huge problems as feral children now roamed the streets during the day as their mothers were at work. And it became a requirement for people to cover their faces when they left their homes.

All these measures were forced through with minimum debate and backed by the threat of fines or imprisonment for infractions.

As a medical practitioner, I was in the front line and I increased the regularity of my visits to the newsagent to stock up on tobacco as far as vagaries of supply allowed as a means of warding off this new disease. But I also followed the newspapers, and I noted that the newspaper which was best informed about the spread of the disease always seemed to be *The Globe*. One had to be early at the shop to get a copy as I was not the only person who had observed this. Because of *The Globe's* early report of the disease in Spain, it had acquired the name, Spanish Flu. *The Globe* was also the first newspaper to make a public reference to this new plague which my rounds of patients told me all too much about, and the first to give the true reason for the increased restrictions on public association.

At eight o'clock one morning in July, I was at Mr Strother's shop and got the last copy. "I'd get extra copies in," he grumbled, "but they limit you on 'ow many you can order wiv newsprint and paper being so short."

When I returned to Queen Square, the maid told me that Mycroft Holmes had come to see me.

"Show him into my consulting room," said I.

"He's there already," said she, and I entered it to find that he had appropriated for himself my consulting chair.

"Your maid let me in, and she brought me in here, as I said I was on important government business," he said without greeting as I entered.

"How can I help you?" I asked, perhaps a little curtly as I confess I was not overly well-disposed to Mycroft Holmes and his unannounced visits.

"I am shortly to put to you a matter of the greatest national importance. Your role in this will be to document the matter under investigation and to give no scintilla of an indication that an investigation is taking place at all to any outsider."

"And what is this matter you wish me to document?"

At that moment there was a knock on the front-door and the sound of footsteps in the hallway. I expected, and I admit my heart leapt at the thought, that it would be my friend, Sherlock Holmes, who would be joining us. But instead, the maid put her head round the door, and said, "A Mr Lestrade to see you, Mr Holmes and Dr Watson."

Inspector Lestrade as pictured by Sidney Paget

"I think you will find that would be Commander Lestrade," came the familiar voice of Lestrade in a slightly chippy tone from the corridor.

Lestrade! I had not seen him in the best part of two decades although I had followed his progress from afar as he climbed the greasy pole of promotion that is the apt description of advancement within a large organization. It had not required any great expertise or persistence by me to follow his professional preferment. For, whatever he may have lacked in investigative skills, the ferret-faced Lestrade more than made up for in his ability to publicise his successes – which for the most part were due to the skills of Sherlock Holmes – and to use the press to allocate the blame to someone else in those investigations – the so-called Jack the Ripper case being the obvious example – where he had been unable to bring the criminal to book.

Even after Holmes's retirement to his beekeeping cottage on the South Downs, Lestrade's ascent through the ranks – from inspector to chief inspector and now to commander and thus just below the rank of the Commissioner of Scotland Yard – had seen him spend vanishingly little time on any of the smaller steps in between.

And here he was before me now in a uniform bristling with emblems and decorations.

"It is good to see you again after all this time, Dr Watson," said he, offering his hand, "and a rare event to be in the company also of Mr Mycroft Holmes."

While I sat on the chair reserved for patients, Lestrade took his position of the additional chair that I kept for the spouse of my patient, and Mycroft Holmes started.

"I have, gentlemen," said Mycroft, "heard of some most disturbing events which although obscure…"

"Is your brother, Mr Sherlock Holmes, not also going to join us?" interrupted Lestrade in a voice tinged with alarm.

"I see no role for him in this," replied Mycroft archly. "This is a matter which requires as much presentational finesse as investigative skill, which is why I would ask that you, Commander Lestrade, work with Dr Watson on it, and why I have not sought to engage my brother."

Lestrade retained his look of extreme concern, but Mycroft continued.

"You are here because I have heard rumours of the most disturbing kind at Downing Street. I am normally only there, you will understand, during the day, as I return to my lodgings in Pall Mall in the evening. As my brother put it, I have my rails and I run on them, and so, after a brief time at my lodgings, I am always at the Diogenes Club from a quarter to five in the evening. But I have heard of matters in Downing Street that would be unthinkable elsewhere in this country."

"What sort of 'matters'?" asked I, at a loss as to what Mycroft might be getting at.

"Parties," said Mycroft simply.

I think my face may have betrayed my feeling of bafflement, and, when I glanced across, I saw a look on Lestrade's face which suggested he felt the same.

"What is there to stage a party for?" asked I, baffled. Although the German spring offensive had ground to a halt, there was no sign of any eastward progress by our forces and the casualty lists remained appallingly high. This, allied to the eruption of this new and virulent illness, made it hard to see anything that might be worth celebrating.

"I confess," said Mycroft, slightly absently, "that the matters we are discussing are not my *métier* in any circumstances. This is where you two gentlemen come in. I would like you to investigate whether so called 'events' took place at all, what form they took, and who took part in them. Was such activity, if it took place, confined to junior staff members who can be summarily dealt with, or did its ramifications extend up to the top of the tree, in which case a decision will have to be taken at a senior level as to what action to take?"

"And how do you propose I should conduct this investigation?" asked Lestrade.

"You have carte blanche," replied Mycroft simply. "You are a commander, so there will be no difficulty in arranging access to Downing Street for you, and you may go and speak to whoever you wish. Dr Watson's record for truthfulness and decency goes before him and no surprise will be expressed by anyone if he takes part in an investigation with Commander Lestrade."

Soon Commander Lestrade and I were walking down Downing Street to interview the staff there. Followers of the accounts I have written of Sherlock Holmes will have seen Lestrade in action as a detective on only a few occasions and never without my friend being present. In the events I described the difference in the investigative talents of the two of them was not so much a gap as a chasm. Where Holmes's talents had the qualities of an epee, Lestrade seemed equipped only with a blunderbuss, and this weapon seemed to spend most of its time pointing at his own feet as he trailed in my friend's wake. I did wonder how Lestrade might deal with an investigation in the absence of Sherlock Holmes. I did not have long to wait.

The official we had been briefed to meet was Sir Godfrey Petherick, the Prime Minister's chief of staff, a formidable figure whom we were introduced to as he sat behind an even more formidable desk.

"We are here to investigate," began Lestrade, "whether there have been any breaches of the government's regulations to control social interactions and hence the spread of the so-called Spanish Flu."

"I would ask you, Commander Lestrade, to make your question more specific. This is a country with a population of thirty million people in a time of a double emergency caused by war and a pestilence. In my capacity as Mr Lloyd George's chief-of-staff, I cannot be expected to know what is happening everywhere in the country."

"My information, Sir Godfrey, is that there were breaches of the anti-pestilence regulations here in Downing Street."

"Commander Lestrade, I do not have time for this. We are waging a war on two fronts. We face Germany and her allies on the battlefield, and there is a deadly contagion that is sweeping the country."

"Were there any gatherings of a social as opposed to of a business nature held in Downing Street?"

"Commander, there are meetings held here all the time." Petherick held up a large desk-diary. "This," he explained, "is the Downing Street appointments book. This shows what meetings are held, in which room, and for what purpose, as well as who attends them. Here," he pointed, "is a reference to the Cabinet meeting in the Cabinet office held at eleven o'clock every Wednesday morning, and here," he pointed again, "is the entry for the Canons and Warheads meeting – you will see that it is often abbreviated to C&W – held every Friday afternoon at half-past-five in the afternoon. And here," he continued, "is the entry for the Bayonets and Ordnance or B&O Committee held on Monday evenings at six."

Lestrade bent over the list.

"The names of the Cabinet members, of course," he said, "I recognise, but who are the people attending the other meetings?"

"Mr Lestrade, 10 Downing Street is a nest of experts in all fields. The politicians who attend Cabinet are there to decide policy while the technical matters are discussed by experts who, while they will not be known to the general public, have insights and knowledge without parallel in their fields."

"There seem to be a lot of experts at the Canon and Warheads committee."

"Between them they would cover weapon design, sourcing of materials, sourcing of manufacture, shipment, and use of the weapons once they are on the battlefield. So, of course, there would be many people required to provide such a wide range of expertise."

"And a lot of the meetings seem to start late in the day."

"There is a war on, Mr Lestrade, and there is a pestilence. 'Late in the day' is not a term I recognise."

Lestrade took another look at the diary.

"The ampersand between the B for Bullets and the O for Ordnance looks more like a Y," he grunted.

"Mr Lestrade, I have heard enough," objected Petherick in a sudden burst of ill-humour. "I cannot imagine that deficiencies in orthography are a matter for police investigation at any time and certainly not at this one. If that is your only remark on this appointments book which is used to control senior level efforts at a time of two national crises, then I think we can consider the matter closed."

A few minutes later saw Lestrade and me at the Diogenes Club. Because of its rule that no member was allowed to speak to or pay the least amount of notice to any other member, this was one of the very few establishments that had been permitted to stay open during the so-called Spanish pestilence. We were shown to the Stranger's Room, the one room of Mycroft's peculiar club where conversation is permitted, and Lestrade told Mycroft of his findings.

"I think," was Mycroft's only response before summarily dismissing us, "that I agree with Sir Godfrey. It is an open and shut case."

"Rather a waste of our time," grunted Lestrade as we headed down the club's stairs. "I won't progress from being Commander with material like that." I was unable to disagree with him on the first comment though, knowing Lestrade's talent for self-publicity, I wondered whether it would be the last of the matter.

I felt my suspicions were justified the following day when I went to Mr Strother's shop. *The Times, The Daily Telegraph*, and *The Daily Mail* led with reports of inappropriate celebrations at Downing Street and the below is a typical example of their output.

> "Fleet Street has been rocked by rumours of jollifications at no less prestigious an address than number 10 Downing Street. Such activities would be misplaced even in the wake of a general election victory, but it would be hard to imagine a greater failure of duty than for such events to take place when the country is confronted both by war and pestilence.
>
> The public has a right to know whether these rumours are justified, and this newspaper will be making the case for a full investigation and disclosure."

The Globe again seemed ahead of its rivals in the investigation. After a paragraph much like the first paragraph of the above, it continued, again under the by-line of Webster Stevenson,

> "I have had an opportunity to conduct my own research into the rumours.
>
> I have been able to establish that no less a personage than Commander George Lestrade, whom our readers will recognise as Inspector Lestrade from his work in some of the most famous cases conducted by Mr Sherlock Holmes,

has already concluded an official investigation into these salacious rumours.

Mr Lestrade has established that no such events took place at all, and the rumours arose because of the need to have meetings at all sorts of unwonted hours in this time of twin emergencies.

The Globe is happy to have set the record straight and wishes that its competitors on Fleet Street had a similar focus on good journalism at this difficult time.

Mr Lestrade is to be congratulated on his work and one wonders what the next step for him is on Scotland Yard's promotional ladder. Sir Troilus Richard, Scotland Yard's Commissioner, and hence the most senior police officer in the country, retires next year. Commander Lestrade must be well-placed to be his successor."

I noted in the days that followed that the rest of the newspapers disassociated themselves from their scandal-infused reportage of the previous days producing modified versions of what *The Globe* had written for its readers.

"There's no doubt that *The Globe*'s ahead of the game," opined Strother when I was next in his shop, "and it shows in its sales."

Like Sir Godfrey Petherick, I considered the matter closed but late in the evening of Friday the 26th of July 1918 there was a tap on the door.

I was unsure whether I would rather the caller be Mycroft Holmes wanting to use my home as his office or a patient suffering from so-called Spanish flu. My reader may imagine my mixture of feelings when I found it was Sherlock Holmes on my doorstep as, for all my joy at seeing my old friend, I could not imagine that his presence was not some harbinger of an assignment that would take me away from my serving my patients.

"My dear fellow," I said, "pray come in."

"You look surprised, and no wonder! Relieved, too, I fancy! I had some supper at Victoria, but I'll smoke a pipe with you with pleasure if you have any tobacco. I could find none in any tobacconist on my way here."

I handed him my pouch, and he seated himself opposite to me and smoked for some time in silence. I knew that only business of importance could have brought him to me at such an hour, and waited patiently until he should come round to it.

"It is like this," he said at length. "I have been given a case by Mycroft of the utmost political delicacy. Tomorrow is the matter's *moment critique* and what I suspect we are about to see is so extraordinary that I need someone as a witness whose name for truth and integrity is unimpeachable."

This sounded remarkably like the most recent matter that Mycroft had petitioned me on, and to which I had been sworn to secrecy, so I held my counsel.

"For the last few weeks," continued Holmes, "I have been working in Downing Street in a number of disguises and I will need to infiltrate it again tomorrow. I can think of no one I would rather have as my witness of what I think I will observe than my good friend Dr Watson."

"And," I asked cautiously, "does Mycroft know you are involving me?"

"He has given me carte blanche to get to the bottom of the matter and, given what I think we will discover, I feel that allows me to turn to you for help."

"Pray continue."

"Tomorrow is a meeting of the Helmets, Berets, Shoes or HBS Committee at 10 Downing Street. The Cabinet Room is booked. I have obtained an invitation with the understanding that I can bring an advisor. I have prepared a business card for you as my advisor going by the name Alfred Draper, and the committee meets in Downing Street at eleven o'clock."

"And what will your alias be?"

"You will hear me introduce myself as Hubert Hatter, millinery expert."

"It will," I said, intrigued as to what I might be witness to, "be an honour to accompany you."

The next day saw us take the short walk to Russell Square Underground Station. The lift down to the platform was full – people about their normal Saturday business augmented by military personnel barracked in Central London but all the travellers, like Holmes and me, were masked with no one talking to each other. We changed at Leicester Square and took the train to the Strand station whence we continued to number 10 Downing Street. Credentials presented, we crossed the threshold of an address almost as famous as that of the quarters Holmes and I used to share at 221 B Baker Street.

There was no doubt as to which room was the Cabinet Room. By contrast with the subdued mood of the Underground, there was an unwonted babble of noise coming out of the first room to the right down the corridor. We entered a room with a large oblong table at its centre and filled with a crowd of people, none of whom was wearing a mask.

I confess, in spite of the babble, I had expected to be entering a room doing business.

Instead at the far side of a table that almost filled the room stood a man with a mane of white hair and a bristling moustache, and just behind him, a short plump man who seemed enwrapped in a haze of cigar smoke. I had seen enough of the boulevard press to know that I was looking at the Prime Minister, Lloyd George, and that the man at his shoulder was the then Munitions Minister, Mr Winston Churchill.

Mr Lloyd George coughed and said, "Gentlemen," in a sonorous Welsh accent followed by, "and Ladies," which he added after a moment's thought as he bowed with a roguish twinkle in his eye to two ladies who stood in the same group on the other side of the table. Then he continued. "He does not yet know why, but heading this way from his official residence at 1 Carlton Gardens is the Foreign Secretary, the estimable Mr Arthur Balfour. We are going to ambush him…" he paused as the door opened and two men in chef's outfits appeared wheeling a trolley crowned by a large metal cloche which the Prime Minister proceeded to remove with a flourish, "with this magnificent cake."

As the Prime Minister was in the process of replacing the cloche, the door sprang open, and another moustachioed figure appeared.

Arthur Balfour

1838-1930

"Foreign Secretary! Mr Balfour!" cried the Prime Minister jovially, "Happy Birthday!" as the assembled gathering broke into a lusty chorus of "Happy Birthday to you." The Prime Minister proceeded to slice the cake and put it onto plates which were passed round among the people present who spilled out into the corridor.

Balfour was, I think, somewhat taken aback by the event prepared in his honour, but he smiled, and addressed the assembled company.

"It has long been an axiom of mine, that nothing matters very much, and few things matter at all. Those without a strategic view of such things, may consider that holding an event such as this is inappropriate in the circumstances in which we find ourselves. But everyone here at the Helmets, Berets, Shoes or HBS Committee..."

"I think you will find that HBS actually stands for Happy Birthday Singing," interjected the Prime Minister in his mellifluous Welsh accent. "It is always desirable to tell the truth about such a subterfuge though seldom, in fact, if ever absolutely necessary..."

"I have always taken more out of drink than drink has taken out of me," murmured Mr Churchill distantly to no one in particular, raising a glass with what looked like whisky to his lips, and swaying slightly as he stood.

"With the twin crises like those with which we are confronted, everyone would be here in Downing Street in any case," continued Balfour at length, "so no one gathered for this welcome serenade is placing themselves or anyone else in any additional danger of contracting this so-called Spanish flu."

"And everyone is working so hard, they deserve a little time when they are not bracing themselves to their duties," added Churchill.

"Of course," added Mr Lloyd George, looking round at the company, "it would be as well if no one here disclosed to someone with less understanding of the finer arts of leadership what has happened here. But if news of our little events does get out, we will of course deny it ever took place."

"I have always gone on the principle that one should never believe anything until it is denied," rejoindered Balfour.

"The greater the truth," responded Lloyd George who had been a highly successful lawyer, "the....

He was about to continue, but I felt a little tug at my sleeve from Holmes and we were soon out in the corridor.

"We must to Sir Godfrey Petherick's room and take his appointments diary as evidence while everyone else in Downing Street is in the Cabinet Room," he whispered. In an instant he had lent action to the word and an instant after that we were back on the pavement of Downing Street.

I think Holmes and I would normally have repaired to a café, but they were of course all closed.

In the end we found a bench in St. James's Park – "This will have to do," said, Holmes, looking slightly warily at the masked passersby hurrying past – where we examined the appointments diary.

"Do you think," I asked, "that C&W really stands for Canons and Warheads?"

"If HBS or Helmets, Berets, Shoes, in fact stands for Happy Birthday Singing, then C&W probably stands for Cheese & Wine. I wonder what Bullets & Ordnance or B&O stands for?"

"The ampersand looks like a Y," I commented. "Could it in fact be Bring Your Own referring to the requirement to bring one's own refreshment?"

"Watson!" exclaimed Holmes, "I do believe you have got it! I flatter myself that the passage of years has not withered my investigative prowess, but it seems to have enabled you to acquire some of your own."

I flushed at this rare word of praise from my friend, although I forbore to say who had originally noted the similarity of the ampersand to a Y.

"We must take this to Mycroft. On a Saturday, he will be at the Diogenes Club," said my friend and a few minutes later saw us in the Stranger's Room of the Diogenes Club.

Mycroft listened closely to Holmes's account of events but interrupted him only when Holmes mentioned the presence of Mr Churchill. "Dear, dear," he murmured, "I had intended Mr Churchill to be the next Prime Minister but three. A discovery such as this with drink, jollity, and ladies present – well, I may be constrained to make other arrangements."

When Holmes finally came to an end, Mycroft exclaimed, "Excellent, Sherlock! I confess I had an idea you might be rather out of your depth on this matter, but you have surpassed yourself in this investigation, although I was not aware you would involve Dr Watson in it."

Mycroft gave me a hard stare, but I looked straight ahead.

"You gave me carte blanche to act on this as I saw fit," said my friend slightly defensively. "Thus, I could not believe that engaging Dr Watson's help would be precluded."

"Indeed not," soothed Mycroft. "Dr Watson has always acted with complete propriety, and I am sure he will do so on this matter also whether I choose to give it any publicity or not."

"Why would you wish to keep a breach of regulations such as this secret?" asked Holmes. "Surely so flagrant a breach of regulations must be met with an appropriate response. It cannot be right that the mass of the population is subject to the most oppressive restrictions while its leaders engage in the liveliest social gatherings."

"Thank you, dear brother," retorted Mycroft with a hint of impatience. "Your expertise, if I may say so, resides in the minutiae of investigations and mine in the larger world of statecraft. You must leave the disposal of this matter to me."

There was a pause as the brothers looked each other in the eye and then Mycroft continued as though there had been no discussion at all.

"I will arrange for this diary to be found in some unexpected place in Downing Street and returned to Sir Godfrey in a way that its absence does not give rise to any suspicion. In quarters as chaotic as number 10 Downing Street is when I am absent, that should not pose any difficulties. Thank you Sherlock and you too Dr Watson, I must now dedicate myself to matters of state."

Although it was not at my friend's request, I travelled to Victoria Station to see Holmes off, and it was some time before I was back at Queen Square. Here I was unsurprised to find Mycroft once again enthroned on the chair in my consulting room.

"Admirably done, dear doctor," he purred, "admirably done – not only with your help to my brother but also with the abstraction of the diary and the aftermath. You are truly the soul of discretion."

"It would," I replied, "be easier to be a soul of discretion, if I understood what was happening."

"These are matters of high state," answered he thoughtfully. "But," he went on, "if I want to involve you again, I suppose it would be as well to provide you with some insight into my workings."

"Pray do so," I said, slightly stiffly.

"I am being blackmailed," said Mycroft simply.

"Blackmailed?" ejaculated I, wondering what secret Mycroft might have, that made him open to blackmail, and why he was choosing to reveal it to me.

"A journalist on *The Globe*, Webster Stevenson, has knowledge that our Prime Minister keeps not only a wife under his roof but also a mistress."

"How can a journalist get so close to the Prime Minister as to know that."

Frances Stevenson

1888 - 1972

"Webster Stevenson is the brother of Frances Stevenson who is the secretary of the Prime Minister. Of the two women you saw at the presentation to Mr Balfour, the Prime Minister's wife was one, and Miss Stevenson was the other. Miss Stevenson, if I may put it this way, takes a broad view of what her duties as the Prime Minister's secretary might require her to fulfil. Her brother has threatened to publish this."

"But the Prime Minister would have to resign if a scandal such as that came out."

"Precisely so. And it is precisely a forced resignation of the Prime Minister that I wish to avoid at this time of twin crises. Webster Stevenson has said that unless I feed his newspaper stories in advance of feeds to other newspapers, he will disclose all. I have been doing this with the result that *The Globe*, rather than being a rather gossipy rag read by the rather gossipy classes, has become the newspaper to turn to first for news. Its circulation at present is constrained only by the availability of newsprint and paper, and Mr Stevenson is the best-known journalist in the country."

"But you have not engaged your brother or me to look into the Prime Minister's affairs?"

"Indeed not, good doctor. There is no need to investigate that as the facts on the Prime Minister's polyamory are indisputable."

"But why have you commissioned two separate investigations into the disgraceful events at Downing Street which have arrived at two diametrically opposed conclusions?"

"I needed to strengthen my hand against the blackmailer. I fed all of Fleet Street the story of the parties in Downing Street. But I commissioned Lestrade to investigate them in the expectation that he would, in his customary way, fail to find out anything of significance. *The Globe* was the only paper that got news of that investigation and so was the first with the story."

"So are you going to take any action on Lestrade's failure to find out the truth?"

"Undoubtedly I will have to do so. When the time is ripe, I will arrange for him to be elevated to be Commissioner of the Metropolitan Police as successor to Sir Troilus Richard. It is useful to have someone in charge there whose investigations have results that are entirely predictable."

"And why did you then commission your brother to make a separate investigation into the matter?"

"If *The Globe* becomes too insistent, I will feed the story of my brother's investigation to another newspaper. When the truth outs, the reputation of the *Globe* as a newspaper of record will be destroyed as it will have got the story totally wrong the first time. Thus, all will be well. On the political front, I suppose I will have to accept that the Prime Minister will then fall from office, and no one will be interested that he is something of a Lothario."

"So you see it as your duty to manipulate events in order to keep the Prime Minister in office or, if you choose, for him to fall?"

"That is what it means, in the words of my brother, for me to *be* the British government."

"And you will make no attempt to bring those who breached Spanish flu regulations in Downing Street to book even though people across the country are being punished for such infractions."

"The Prime Minister is in politics which is by its very nature transient. I am in government which by its very nature has no other purpose than permanence. I would only use the events you refer to, if by doing so I contributed to the smooth running of the ship of state."

As my reader may imagine, I kept a close eye on the press over the next few weeks. I was used to them carrying reports of the military triumphs or disasters, but I wondered in particular what story *The Globe* might publish next.

In fact, the matters above were rapidly overtaken by events.

Webster Stevenson succumbed to the Spanish flu early in August 1918. Without Stevenson's ability to obtain stories ahead of the rest of Fleet Street, *The Globe's* sudden pre-eminence swiftly waned, and it was eventually closed in 1922. The summer of 1918 is also the start of what became known as the hundred days which brought the Great War to a triumphant end. By 1940, Mr Churchill had sufficiently advanced in Mycroft's favour, that he did indeed become the Prime Minister, although the disapproval Churchill had attracted from Mycroft may have had the result that Churchill became the next Prime Minister but four rather than the next Prime Minister but three as Mycroft had originally intended.

For myself, I was pleased to be able to dedicate myself to the care of my patients.

And it was with pleasure on the 19th of July 1919, the day victory in the Great War just past was celebrated, that I saw a hale Miss Pendry smoking a Woodbine with an air of calm and practised assurance. She was walking arm in arm down Southampton Row with a soldier on leave whom I recognised as the newly demobilised Sergeant Billings who was puffing contentedly at his pipe.

Afterword by Henry Durham

This account of events from the pen of Dr Watson would have been dismissed as even less believable than the most incredible of his canonical works were it not for the almost complete repetition of them by the British Prime Minister Boris Johnson during the Corona virus crisis of 2020 to 2022 the end of which coincided with the outbreak of war in Ukraine. Johnson shared Lloyd George's voracious appetite for mistress as well as his love for exuberant living. The main difference between the events described here and events in so called "Partygate" is that Lloyd George's parties (though not his other appetites) have remained a secret until now whereas Partygate was one of the factors that led to Boris Johnson's resignation.

It is perhaps unsurprising that Mycroft Holmes, master of political statecraft that he was, was able to keep parties at Downing Street at a time of supreme crisis in 1918 out of the public eye while his twenty-first century successors as advisors to the Prime Minister were unable to do the same. It is for readers to decide whether the failure of Mycroft Holmes's successors at Downing Street to suppress news of such matters is to their benefit.

EPISODE IV

The Art of the Possible – Introduction by Mycroft Holmes

The matter that follows is the most significant that I handled in my career serving the British government, for this narrative covers my arrangement of the Armistice which ended the Great War but a few years ago. While it is I who retell the events that led up to the signing of the Armistice in November 1918, I leave the retelling of the story of my time in the Netherlands, German-occupied Belgium, and France to the good Dr Watson whose record as a reporter speaks for itself.

War, as we have seen in *A Modern Odysseus* can flare up as if from nowhere, but once men and arms have been staked on a successful outcome, concluding it requires that even the vanquished get something out of the final negotiations, and that even the victors do not to get everything they sought. As any future reader will find out, this is not the same thing as saying the defeated belligerent gets any of what he originally sets out to achieve. The key point is to find a way of getting him to accept terms when he might otherwise fight on and the key point with the victorious party is getting him to forgo some of the spoils of his triumph. The reader will discover within what follows what will persuade the victor or the vanquished to do this.

The basis of the final settlement was the so-called Fourteen Points promulgated by the American President Woodrow Wilson. They are summarised below:

1. Open diplomacy without secret treaties
2. Economic free trade on the seas during war and peace
3. Equal trade conditions
4. Decrease of armaments among all nations
5. Adjustment of colonial claims
6. Evacuation of Germany and its allies from Russia
7. Restoration of Belgium in its former boundaries
8. Return of all French territories taken in the Franco-Prussian war of 1871.
9. Readjustment of Italian borders
10. Self-determination for Austria-Hungary
11. Creation of Romania, Serbia and Montenegro
12. Creation of a Turkish state with guaranteed free trade in the Dardanelles
13. Creation of an independent Polish state
14. Creation of the League of Nations

Points 1 to 3 were objectionable to any victorious party as they would limit his freedom of action to dispose of victory as he chose. Points 4, 5, 9, and 14 were so vague as to be meaningless. Points 6, 10, 11, 12, and 13 were of no great relevance to Great Britain and France without whose agreement there would be no end to hostilities, while points 7 and 8 would be decided by military realities.

None of this was my concern.

My objective was to get all parties to sign up to them as the basis for peace and the below relates how I achieved this. During the course of this, I met the closest I got to a counterpart in my career but, though his skills were at my level, he had the misfortune of holding a Yarborough hand of cards whereas I held all the aces.

The Art of the Possible - Part 1 by Mycroft Holmes

George Clemenceau

1849 - 1921|

"Fourteen! Fourteen!"

The walrus-like moustache of my seventy-seven-year-old visitor, the French Prime Minister Georges Clemenceau, quivered with anger as he stood before me in my office in Whitehall. "The American President's proposal for ending this war has fourteen points!" he went on, his show of emotion unabated. "The good Lord managed to limit himself to ten points when he was telling the world what to do. Mais non! Ça ne suffit pas pour Monsieur le Président."

Although, like my brother, Sherlock, I speak French, Clemenceau translated to make his meaning clear. "But that is not enough for Mr Woodrow Wilson when he takes it upon himself to do the same as the Almighty. I am an old man, Mr Holmes, but I must own that it is my wish that I could pass water with the same fluency as that man can speak."

It was Monday the 4th of November 1918, and Clemenceau – unusually for a Frenchman, a fluent English speaker as he had spent time in America – was on a secret mission to London to discuss the progress of the war.

"But," responded I, "the substance of President Wilson's Fourteen Points means the German occupying forces will leave France, and the territories of the Alsace and the Lorraine will be returned to France after their annexation by the Germans in 1871. Moreover, Germany and Austria will be weakened beyond recognition as their empires are broken into countries run by their constituent peoples as Poland, Czechoslovakia, and Hungary are established as independent nations. Surely that is what you want."

"That is not even the beginning of what I want. My country has been laid to waste by the German invasion. A third of it, including all the industrialised parts, is still in their hands, and you can be sure that they will sabotage anything of any value if they leave it. And we have lost one and a half million men, not to mention another million and a half wounded. We will need to pay war pensions for the next seventy years and our coffers are empty. Yet for all the vacuities in Mr Wilson's Fourteen Points, there is no mention of reparations and no mention of punishment for those who visited this catastrophe on us."

"What do you want me to do?" I asked.

"When my American wife was unfaithful to me, Mr Holmes," replied Clemenceau, not answering my question, "I had her put into prison, stripped of her French citizenship, and then deported back to America. And I made sure she sailed steerage and that she never had any more contact with our children."

"I see."

"That is as nothing compared to what I want to do to the Germans. The Kaiser should be put on trial and hanged. And I want to annex the west bank of the Rhine. We have an offensive planned in the Alsace under the commander-in-chief of our army, Marshal Pétain, to enforce it. He will march to the German border and onward to the west bank of the Rhine. That is the way we will secure our borders. Not with mealy-mouthed good intentions."

"You make yourself very plain."

"I know your role as the British Government, Mr Holmes. Your brother, Sherlock, may have won a Légion d'honneur for stopping the Boulevard assassin, but in your position you are far more powerful than he. You must make your Prime Minister see that what is in my country's interest is in the interests of this one. I want for Germany reparation, subjugation, and emasculation. And you English should want the same."

And with that imperative, this whirl of energy – not for nothing known as "le tigre" or "the tiger" – stormed from my office.

I set myself to reading military despatches that had come in from the various fronts for I suspected I would not be left undisturbed for long. For the first time since the war began, the news from the various fronts was almost uniformly good, as Germany's allies – Austria-Hungary, Bulgaria, and Turkey – were all suing for peace. But, as I had anticipated, the Prime Minister of Great Britain, Lloyd George, was the next caller at my office.

"I take it," said the Prime Minister, with an unwonted lack of preamble, "that my French counterpart has expressed his concerns to you about Mr Wilson's Fourteen Points."

I nodded my assent.

"I confess I have misgivings about them of my own. The first point is about there being no secret protocols to treaties."

"What of it?"

"The Italians were originally allied with the Austrians, and we would not have them on our side in this war if the treaties we have with them did not contain secret protocols giving them additional territories to those we have said they should have. It was most imprudent of Dr Watson to disclose our use of such protocols in *The Naval Treaty*. Secret treaties and secret protocols are the stuff of diplomacy at which we…" – and here he nodded at me and corrected himself – "you, are a master. I would not want my hand circumscribed in that area."

"Anything else?"

The President's second point of the fourteen calls on economic freedom of the seas in war and in peace. For all the millions of lives we have lost on front after front, it has been our blockading of the German ports that has been by far the most successful stratagem in throttling the life out of them. And by comparison this has hardly cost us anyone. It would be very hard to sign up to abjuring the ability to do that."

"What is it you wish me to do?"

Rather in contrast to the drooping moustache of Prime Minister Clemenceau, the trim moustache of Prime Minister Lloyd George, now twitched perkily upwards.

"For all my reservations about these points, I have no wish that this bloodbath should continue for a minute longer than is necessary to achieve an acceptable solution. The Americans have intimated to us that the Germans may be inclined to accept the

President's Fourteen Points as a basis for a settlement of this war. Let us therefore seek to give effect to this. Or, to be more precise, I wish that it be you who gives effect to this. The German supreme military headquarters is at Spa in occupied Belgium and that is where the Kaiser and his main ministers are at present. I want you to go to Spa and ensure that they sign up."

"What powers do I have?"

"You may do as you see fit. Your role is to ensure that the Germans and the French sign. I want nothing more than to be the first political leader among the western allies to be able to stand before his people's representatives in Parliament and announce the war is over at last."

"And the Kaiser?"

The Prime Minister hesitated. "His first cousin, our King George V, has described the Kaiser as the greatest criminal in the world. Yet he remains the grandson of the last queen. To see someone of that lineage at a capital and public trial would be very difficult. And there is no knowing what royal secrets he might disclose. We British have no interest in seeing him in the dock."

"And how will I get to Spa?"

"There is a car waiting outside to take you to your flat in Pall Mall where you may pick up your impedimenta. The car will then go to Dr Watson's house in Queen Square where he has been told to stand by. If he is a witness, no one will think to challenge the version of events that is published. The two of you will then be taken to Harwich where a merchant ship will take you to the Hoek of Holland. You should be in Spa by Thursday."

The Art of the Possible - Part 2 by Dr Watson

Once more the game was afoot yet in my bones I felt only foreboding.

Was the war that had raged inch by inch across Belgium and eastern France for four years at last coming to an end? For all that the news had been much better in recent weeks, who was I to know if this improvement would be sustained? And yet here I was, off to the German military headquarters in Belgium at the command of the Prime Minister.

Queen Wilhelmina

1880 - 1962

The journey was a long one, and Mycroft Holmes, my companion in this journeying, was even less given to conversation than his brother. It was thus a relief to spend Tuesday night in the Hague at the court of the Dutch monarch Queen Wilhelmina.

Over a paltry repast, made even more difficult by the presence of Queen Wilhelmina's German husband, I was curious to find out how the Dutch had been able to avoid the German occupation which had been the fate of their Belgian and

Luxembourg neighbours. I put this to the redoubtable Dutch monarch.

"The Kaiser did threaten me with occupation when he came here on a visit," replied she brightly but with a determined jut of the chin. "He said that his soldiers are two metres tall. But I told my little cousin, that if one of his two-metre-tall soldiers set a single toe in my country, I would open the dykes and the whole place would disappear under three metres of water. The motto of our royal house is, 'I will maintain'. And if, to maintain my country's independence I am forced to launch a flood which makes Noah's flood look like a passing shower, then that is what I will do."

I noted her husband look stony-faced at this aperçu and was glad that he refrained from making any comment. "And irrespective of the nationality or height of the soldiers in question," she added firmly, her chin jutting out again, "I would say the same to the ruler of any other power that sought to push me around."

Thursday morning found us in Spa.

In retrospect, Spa, south-east of Brussels, was an obvious place for the Germans to have their supreme quarters.

As the place's name suggests, it is a place where in happier times the wealthy go to take the waters, and so has a plentiful supply of imposing buildings to requisition for military use, as well as good railway connections in all directions. The town had been captured largely undamaged by the Germans in 1914 and, even in wartime, with the normally white-stuccoed walls of the buildings painted khaki, it was a most agreeable place ringed by tree-topped hills. The Kaiser himself was housed in a grandiose villa called Villa du Neubois although, as we awaited his arrival in an imposing reception room, it was impossible not to be feel the ground shudder as the air was rent by the reports of artillery fire, for all that the front was over one hundred miles away.

Kaiser Wilhelm II

1859 - 1941

While King George V's disinclination to speak and his austerity of manner were legendary. Wilhelm II, his Prussian cousin was known for being flamboyant of gesture despite having a foreshortened left arm which was capable of little more than hanging limply at his side and which gave him a distinctly unbalanced look, exacerbated when, as now, he chose to strut up and down before us as he spoke.

"I am not sure I would like to go on with these Fourteen Points of President Wilson's now that I have given the matter some thought," he started, puffing at an enormous cigar.

"You mean," protested Mycroft, with a show of emotion that was quite unwonted for him, "that we have made this journey from London to Spa for you to tell us that you do not after all want to discuss terms to end the war."

The Kaiser gave a lopsided shrug. "I see myself as a victim of conflicting advice. My main military advisor or quartermaster general was Erich Ludendorff and he told me to keep fighting till we have victory. And before that he had told me that the war was lost having promised me victory in the spring. He is always changing his mind. So why should not I?"

We seemed to have reached an impasse.

"American troops are landing in Europe at a rate of two-hundred-thousand a month," ventured Mycroft.

"But my generals tell me they are raw by contrast with the battle-hardened troops we are able to bring to the West now that our war with Russia is at an end."

"The population of America is three times yours. I suspect the Americans can land an additional two-hundred-thousand soldiers a month for longer than you can draft in soldiers from your Eastern front," Mycroft Holmes retorted. "And with every month that passes, the American troops who are already here become less raw."

His sally was met by silence and the Prime Minister's Permanent Special Advisor continued.

"May I ask the Kaiser why he is here in Spa rather than in Berlin, the seat of government of his Empire? And why he should be seeing me on his own when he attaches such weight to the opinion of his generals?"

At that moment the door flew open and a man in military uniform who looked young and vigourous for what I later found out to be fifty-five years burst in.

"Ah, Mr Holmes," said the Kaiser to Mycroft, "this is Wilhelm Groener. He is the quartermaster general in succession to Ludendorff whom I have already dismissed."

"Even though you have accepted Ludendorff's view on the advisability or otherwise of continuing the war?" asked Mycroft.

Wilhelm Groener

1867 - 1939

"I find it helps to keep my staff on their toes," replied the Kaiser with a casual wave of his cigar, and, turning to Groener, barked, "Well?"

"Your Majesty," came a stuttering reply, "it is coming through on the wires that there is revolution in Berlin. And it is spreading across Germany. The Social Democrats are calling for your abdication as a way of preventing a Bolshevist takeover of the government."

"Bolshevists! I am being betrayed by my own people!" exclaimed the Kaiser, his eyes widening. "They did for my cousin in Russia. And they will do for me here if they get half a chance. I thought I could stop this sort of thing happening by giving the people a parliament. Even though it is I who still takes all the big decisions."

He took a long puff at his cigar.

"Maybe I should dissolve the people and choose myself another." He paused to muse on this remark before turning his gaze to Groener once more. "Or perhaps, rather than wasting time in discussion with Mr Mycroft Holmes, I should return to Berlin now and quell the revolution myself."

"The revolutionaries are already in control of the crossings over the Rhine. I cannot guarantee your safety if you do as you suggest," interjected Groener.

The Kaiser's face fell.

"What do you recommend I should do, Groener?"

"The honourable course for His Majesty," replied Groener looking slightly evasive, "would be if he were to head to the front, mount a horse, and lead a final charge against the enemy. I have been able to get together a fleet of cars to take him there."

"You have got together a fleet of cars? I thought we had run out of everything," exclaimed the Kaiser. He turned to Mycroft. "And what do you recommend, Mr Holmes?" asked the Kaiser, turning to Mycroft.

"My brief is to clarify for you anything in President Wilson's Fourteen Points that would prevent you making terms on the basis of them. I am not here to provide you with personal advice."

"I note that I am not personally mentioned in the President's points."

"Peace on Mr Wilson's Fourteen Points is about principles, Your Majesty. It is not about personalities."

"When my air force was bombing London, I instructed them not to drop bombs west of Charing Cross Station to avoid endangering my relatives. Surely that was showing principles and respecting personalities."

"How you might wish to defend yourself in a potential war-crimes trial is a matter for you."

"A war-crimes trial you say?" – this asked in an aghast whisper.

And before anyone had a chance to say anything else, the emperor had turned on his heel and stridden from the room to leave Mycroft and me alone with Groener.

Groener and Mycroft eyed each other.

"How much of what you have said is true?" asked Mycroft, I think curious as to how Groener could have made such a convenient interjection.

"All of it, Mr Holmes."

"And can you do anything about this insurrection?"

"The armed forces will obey me, Mr Holmes, if I ask them to put it down. They will obey me as long as the orders I give them are not completely deranged."

"Your Navy at Kiel mutinied last week."

"They had been given orders to set sail to take on the much bigger British Navy in the English Channel. And we had no ammunition to give them. We Germans are, for the most part, brave. But even those of us whose grasp of reality is perhaps not quite what it should be, or whose bravery is perhaps not quite what they say it is, are not, as you have seen, suicidal."

"But how will you control the rest of your armed forces?"

At that moment the door opened again and in came a man whose uniform was weighed down with military medals.

Paul von Hindenburg

1847 - 1934

"This is Field Marshal Paul von Hindenburg, supreme commander of the German Imperial army," said Groener. "And, in answer to your question, Mr Holmes, I am in talks with the Social Democrat leader, Friedrich Ebert. I have offered him the use of the army to stop the Bolshevists from taking power. In return he will leave me in charge of the army once he has assumed office. The Field Marshal here," Groener nodded in Hindenburg's direction, "has expressed the wish to retire to civilian life once this conflict is over. Our army operates separately from the rest of the Reich and has its own institutions and procedures. Being in charge of it gives the office-holder almost the same power as being the Reich's Chancellor."

"The army of which you will then be in charge?" Mycroft asked Groener. "Meaning that you will have the same powers as the political leader of Germany?"

"I repeat, the Field Marshal here is the army's supreme commander," Groener replied, again sounding slightly evasive.

"And the Fourteen Points?" pressed Mycroft.

"As I said, there is a convoy of cars on its way. It carries a delegation from Berlin. I will not weary you with the party's precise make up, but it will be led by Matthias Erzberger, a member of our parliament who has been calling for peace talks for some time. The delegation has been given the responsibility of negotiating a cease-fire on the terms of the Fourteen Points to which you refer."

Erzberger was a name unknown to me and evidently also to Mycroft and he asked Groener for more details.

"He is in the government as a minister without portfolio. He has been there for a month."

"You are using a minister without direct responsibility for anything and who has only just joined your government to sign a peace accord?" exclaimed Mycroft in some surprise. "Does it not fall to you, as supreme commander of the army," he continued, turning to Hindenburg, "to lead the delegation?"

"I have always taken the view that negotiating matters such as this is best left to politicians," said Hindenburg with a shrug. "Politicians decide the policy. Soldiers try to provide the means to deliver on that policy. It is not untrue to say that war is politics by other means."

"It might ease matters all around, Mr Holmes, if, in the absence of the leader of our army, you and Dr Watson were to accompany Erzberger and the rest of his party," said Groener.

"You want me to accompany your German delegation to peace talks?" asked Mycroft Holmes looking somewhat taken aback.

"I think you might have a role as a communicator between us and the French."

"How have you been able to agree all of this with the government in Berlin from here in Spa when there is a revolution in Germany?"

"I had a secret telephone line installed in the Reich Chancellery which I am making use of to talk to directly to Ebert."

"And why are you facilitating this?"

Groener looked into the distance. "We Germans have fought this war as far as we can. People at home are starving and this winter will be cold as there is no fuel for household heating. At the front, our forces are ill-supplied with everything to wage war. My background is in the railways, so I know the supply situation. If you cannot supply your troops, the struggle is senseless."

I could see that Mycroft was somewhat at a loss for words at this rational attitude. I think Groener saw this, and he continued. "We need a new way of doing things and maybe a new way of governing ourselves."

A light came into Groener's eyes as though he were having a vision.

"Perhaps," he continued eventually, "in the years to come, a German government can be chosen by its people in a proper democratic process, and we will not find ourselves in thrall to a man whose judgment," – he broke off and glanced at the door through which the Kaiser had exited – "is so questionable."

"What is to happen next?" asked Mycroft.

"In an hour the convoy of cars I referred to will draw up outside this villa. A point to cross the battle-lines has been agreed with the French. This is at La Capelle, ten miles inside France. On our side a bugler will play the cease-fire call and the leading driver will wait until he hears the French response."

"And you are in accordance with all of this?" Mycroft asked, turning to Hindenburg.

"I would refer you to my previous remarks," replied the German Imperial Army's Supreme Commander, and withdrew from the room as abruptly as he had entered it.

"I think Pontius Pilate could have learnt a thing or two from our Field Marshal," said Groener with a shrug. But Groener proved he was a man of his word, for precisely an hour after our discussions, seven cars had drawn up outside Villa Neubois.

"You are safest, gentlemen," said Groener to us, "if you sit in the sixth car."

"Why not the seventh? Surely the rearmost car is safest," I queried.

"Only the first six are part of the delegation. The seventh car will stay here."

"You are truly a man after my own heart," said Mycroft to Groener with a warmth in his voice I had never previously heard and, to my astonishment, he embraced the German.

Matthias Erzberger

1875 -1921

Discussions had come to an end, and we got into the sixth car. I found myself sitting next to a gloom-laden man in his mid-forties who introduced himself to me as Matthias Erzberger and who had the air of a somewhat doleful bank-clerk.

"I have a brief that will destroy the Reich," he repeated. "I will be remembered as the man who betrayed his country. I don't know what will happen to me when I return."

"Your country is tired of war," replied Mycroft. "That is why your people have risen in rebellion. Surely making peace on the best terms you can get is better than this ceaseless slaughter. Once Germany has made peace, it can once more join the family of nations. That is what the League of Nations is all about. And Woodrow Wilson's Points propose ideals which a future statesman should be proud to sign up to."

"A future statesman, eh?" replied Erzberger perking up. "I must own I have been called many worse things than that! And I am a newcomer to this governing business, so I was quite surprised to be made leader of this delegation. At the start of the war, I saw it only as an opportunity and called for territorial annexations. But over the last two years, I have been calling for peace. Maybe my change to being a man of peace was worth it after all."

"It is the mark of a statesman to be able to adjust his views to circumstance."

Erzberger said nothing at my words but sat upright in his seat with his chest puffed up. I could hear him saying, "A statesman, eh?" to himself over and over again.

We set off, and even through the closed car windows and over the noise of the engines, we could hear artillery fire although the mellow autumnal countryside and the pretty red-brick villages which the Germans had taken without much of a fight a few years previously were quite unspoilt in the land we were traversing. But the further along the one-hundred-and-thirty-mile journey west we got, the more we could see how stray shells and mortars had done their work with half-repaired shell-holes in the roads, and the surrounding fields raddled and pitted.

At five miles short of the agreed crossing point, the road became impossible to follow.

"We will have to try our luck going over the mud," said our driver.

After a few minutes of driving at a snail's pace, we came to a halt.

And then a man in the field-grey uniform of the German army and with a bugle hanging from his side ran up to us. "There is a cease-fire for half an hour and so you may pass through. Our lines and those of the French are about four-hundred metres apart here."

The land we now traversed is not called No-man's Land for nothing.

Where Spa had been ringed by wooded hills, here there was no discernible feature on the desolate landscape around us. Artillery had scoured it of any vegetation longer than coarse grass, and we could hear the reports of mortars, shells, and what else I knew not, from either side of the section of the front not covered by the cease-fire. The only features were water-filled craters and the rotting cadavers of men and horses, the only movements came from rats the size of small dogs which scuttled around gorging themselves on dead and decaying flesh. The vermin were so engrossed in this that they were not frightened off by our car. Our drivers had to swerve crazily to find terrain it was possible to drive on and it was only after many a slip that we eventually came to the French lines. As we did so, a rocket went up, and we were no more than a few hundred lines behind the French lines when the firing started up again in all its fury.

We were stopped by a sentry. "Drive on a hundred metres and a motorcyclist will overtake you. Your convoy should follow him," he instructed.

The next half an hour was like the journey up to the front of the German lines, as featureless expanses of mud flanked us. But then we came to the first French village behind the front which had been in German hands until only a few days previously. All that remained standing was the burnt-out stump of the church spire while the ground showed the outlines of where houses had once stood but did so no longer. We passed through one village after another, all similar or worse. Sometimes we would pass through what had been woodland but of which the only surviving remnants were stumps charred down to ground level.

"This will be awful … awful," wailed Erzberger.

"Are there no German territories in a similar state?" I could not forebear to ask, knowing that no allied troops had got anywhere near German territory and so Germany was entirely undamaged.

Erzberger stared ahead.

"Where are they taking us?" he asked querulously over and over again.

We were not destined to find out for some time, as the French motorcyclist took us on a journey which lasted through the night.

"Surely we have been here before," said Erzberger as we passed through yet another shattered village as dawn on the next day was breaking.

I was too wearied and confused by our nocturnal journey to answer, although I was to establish afterwards that as the crow flies our journey was not more than forty miles. Eventually, after what by my watch had been ten hours, our car journey came to an end at a railway siding where a train with a locomotive and two Wagons-Lits carriages was waiting.

"You should board this," said our guide. "It will take you to your final destination."

"I fear the worst," repeated Erzberger as we set off for what was to prove to be another hour of journeying until our train drew to a halt.

A French soldier banged on the window and signalled we should get down.

We found ourselves on twin tracks in a woodland clearing. One-hundred-and-fifty yards away on a stretch of mud over which a wooden walkway had been laid stood another short train with cannons mounted on flat trucks at both ends.

Erzberger led his delegation, which Mycroft and I were now a part of, over to the other train.

Waiting for us was another delegation – I noted both French and British uniforms amongst them.

Ferdinand Foch

1851 - 1929

The moustached man who led it stepped forward. "I am Marshal Foch," he said. "May I ask you gentlemen, what brings you here?" he asked, disregarding Erzberger's proffered hand.

"We are here to hear your proposals for ending this war," replied Erzberger.

"I am only authorised to give you those if I have your confirmation you are seeking an armistice. Are you seeking an armistice?"

"Yes, we are seeking an armistice."

"I am afraid you will need to speak a little louder, gentlemen."

"Yes, we are seeking an armistice."

"Just a little louder again please, gentlemen."

"Yes, we are seeking an armistice," responded Erzberger, almost in a shout.

"Very well," said Foch. "I am the Supreme Commander of Allied Forces. Where is the Supreme Commander of the German army?"

"I have been sent in his stead and with his authority."

"I see. And have you full signing powers?"

"Yes."

"Then here are our terms," said Foch, handing over a sheaf of documents. "You may take them or leave them. If you leave them, the war will continue. And the war will in any case continue while you consider them."

"When shall we meet for further discussions?"

"There are no further discussions. You have seventy-two hours to sign these proposals. After that you will be taken back to your lines."

"What if I need to confer with Berlin?"

"I thought you said you had full signing powers?"

"I may need to consult on the practicalities of what is required."

"We will provide telegraphic services."

"Then you will know what we are saying."

"That is not my problem. I have nothing further to say to you."

And Foch turned on his heel and climbed up the little ladder into his train.

He was just about to go back into the carriage when Mycroft Holmes stepped forward.

"I am Mycroft Holmes, the Permanent Special Advisor to the British Prime Minister."

I forbore to identify myself but Foch fixed Mycroft with a stare.

"That sounds like someone more worthy of the attention of the Supreme Commander of the Allied Forces. Very well. You may raise any questions of detail with me, but the substance of these armistice proposals is not negotiable."

We retired with Erzberger and his party to our side of the clearing to review the proposals that he had been handed.

"I don't even know if it possible to meet these demands," said the German politician gloomily after a first read. "We are being required to evacuate all occupied territories everywhere within two weeks. All territory on the west bank of the Rhine will be occupied by the allied armies. A strip of territory six miles wide on the east bank of the Rhine will be made a neutral zone. That will mean we will have to abandon all our positions and move all our forces across to the other side of the river and then another six miles eastwards."

"You have asked for an armistice. Is that not what you should expect? The alternative is that you will have to retreat and be routed in that retreat. The proposals allow you to withdraw your forces in good order. That is surely a better alternative and one you can sell to your people."

"But as well as surrendering 5,000 pieces of light and heavy artillery, 25,000 machine guns, 3,000 mortars, and 1,700 aeroplanes, we are required to surrender 5,000 locomotives, 150,000 railway cars, and 5,000 motor lorries. That we shall be disarmed, I understand. But how will we move our forces without any means of transport? I will have to telegraph Groener to find out if this is possible."

The telegram was sent, and the message came back from Groener, "Four weeks needed to evacuate. Otherwise we risk an attack from the rear and our men will be on foot with no weapons."

"We have no choice but to ask for an extension," said Erzberger. He looked at the conditions again. "And they are asking for us give them 200 submarines. We don't even have that many in our fleet."

There was a long pause.

"Mr Holmes," said Erzberger, "maybe you can come with me to make a case to Marshal Foch that this is impractical or impossible."

Erzberger, Mycroft, and I went across to the other train.

We stood on the wooden duckboards and a man in a British naval uniform came to the platform at the entrance. I was subsequently to learn that he was the First Lord of the Admiralty, Rosslyn Wemyss.

Erzberger made his points about the withdrawal of forces and of the time period allowed for it and the impossibility of surrendering 200 submarines. He handed the British official his copy of the documents detailing the armistice terms and Wemyss disappeared inside the carriage to emerge a couple of minutes later carrying the same document with the "200" before the word "submarines" struck out and replaced by the word, "All".

"And the Marshal says that all logistical problems are matters you will need to solve," said Wemyss.

The process of the German delegation going to Foch's train, asking for concessions, and being told that it was not a negotiation continued over the next three days. In the end, Erzberger turned to Mycroft and said, "Can we have one more attempt to give us more time to withdraw our troops, Mr Holmes? We have a revolution in Germany, and he wants most of our railway stock. Maybe it would help if just you and Dr Watson went."

I do not think even a man so free of self-doubt as Mycroft was sure about the propriety of this, but I assume he considered it his duty to try to get both the Entente and the Central Powers to end the bloodshed. He and I were eventually admitted to see Foch.

"You, Mr Holmes," said Foch to Mycroft, "I will talk to. I confess I see no reason to be reasonable with the Germans. I have lost a son and my daughter has lost her husband. And after this slaughter she will find it hard to find another."

"If you push the Germans too far, the war will continue, and more lives will be lost."

"So be it. I will gather my resources and then I will force the Germans back further until I get all the way to the west bank of the Rhine."

"Really?" replied Mycroft blandly. "I thought the next offensive was to be launched by your colleague Marshal Pétain, whose forces are further to the south."

"What!" exclaimed Foch, "This is the first I have heard of this! Though I was always had my suspicions. So, Clemenceau is giving Pétain the chance to steal the glory of the final victory. It is the troops under my command here in the north who have made most of the recent advances and I am the Supreme Commander of Allied Forces. I see no reason why someone of Pétain's rank should get all the credit. Very well. Let us give the Germans a month rather than two weeks to withdraw their forces if that is what they need."

We went back to Erzberger and Mycroft told him the concession he had got for him.

"In the meantime," said Erzberger, "I have got a telegram from Hindenburg. This is what he has to say." Erzberger read out: "'Groener says our army cannot offer meaningful resistance. You should sign even if the terms cannot be improved – Hindenburg.'"

"At least this concession will mean you have got something, as you will be able to withdraw your troops in good order," I said to Erzberger as we set off to Foch's train just at the first glimmering of dawn on the 11th of November.

We had knocked on the side of the carriage and were waiting for someone to speak to us when a thought occurred to Erzberger. He exclaimed: "I did not check what matters were not in the terms of the armistice. And I now realise that the terms make no mention of the lifting of the blockade."

By now Foch and his contingent were filing out onto the little platform on the end of the carriage.

"Will you sign?" asked Foch.

"If I do so, will you lift the blockade?"

"That is not in the terms I have given you. The terms lay obligations on Germany. There are no obligations on anyone else."

"The main people suffering from the blockade are women and children and they are starving."

"I don't recall U-Boat captains worrying too much about the suffering of British women and children when they were torpedoing our cargo ships," piped up Wemyss, who was on the little platform above us beside Foch.

"I thought the second of Wilson's points called for free passage on the seas."

"I think I have a solution," said Foch, and Erzberger's face brightened.

"I will," continued Foch, "add to the terms we have offered you a clause which specifies that the blockade will not be lifted until a final treaty is signed. Then the matter is clear. I would add, Herr Erzberger, that in the territories we have liberated from German occupation, the inhabitants have told us that you Germans left them to starve."

He paused to let his words to sink in before asking, "And when would you like hostilities to end?"

"As soon as possible to prevent unnecessary loss of life," said Erzberger.

"Would you be able to tell your troops by one o'clock?" asked Mycroft.

"Sooner than that," said Erzberger.

"Ah, I forgot," said Foch. "Our advances mean your lines of communication are getting shorter by the hour. Let us say eleven o'clock."

"Every hour we delay, costs mo –" began Erzberger.

But Wemyss interrupted, "We could refer to it as happening at the eleventh hour of the eleventh day of the eleventh month.

Foch seemed quite taken by Wemyss's remark.

"Eleven o'clock it is," the Marshal declared.

There seemed nothing further to say and Erzberger and his delegation climbed into the French railway carriage. "Before I sign, I must make a final protest about the harshness of the terms," said Erzberger, pen poised above the signature page.

"Very well. You have protested," said Foch and shrugged. "Now sign."

"A nation of seventy million people may suffer," said Erzberger, as he eventually applied his pen, "but it does not die."

"Very well," said Foch again and gave another shrug before disregarding another attempt by Erzberger to shake his hand.

Our role in the German party had come to an end. Erzberger looked utterly downcast at his failure to get any more concessions out of Foch, but Mycroft had a special word for him. "Statesmanship is a difficult skill," he said, "but your name is on this agreement and that shows you are a man to be trusted with important commissions. And President Wilson's Fourteen Points envisage a League of Nations to resolve future disputes. Germany will need to be represented there by someone of substance."

Pointing out the responsibility that was being bestowed on him again seemed to cheer Erzberger, who re-boarded his train with his delegation and departed while Mycroft Holmes and I joined a convoy of vehicles bound for Paris.

By ten o'clock Foch, Mycroft Holmes and I were in the office of Georges Clemenceau.

Foch handed Clemenceau the signed Armistice agreement.

"Admirable! Admirable!" purred 'le tigre', and he embraced us in turn, before – and it pains me to say this – he planted a kiss on the cheeks of each of Foch, Mycroft, and me. "You gentlemen have delivered peace to me at exactly the right time to enable me to make an announcement in the Parliament when it opens in an hour."

At that moment there was a knock on the door and in came yet another moustached figure.

Philippe Pétain

1856 - 1951

"I am come," said a man, who I was told was Marshal Philippe Pétain, "to advise the Prime Minister of the final arrangements for the next offensive which will secure for us German territories all the way up to the Rhine."

"There will be no need for such an offensive. We are already celebrating the end of the war," said Clemenceau airily. "I have in my hand a piece of paper on which the Germans have signed up to our terms."

"My felicitations," said Pétain coldly. "I take it that the agreement hands the west bank of the Rhine to France, obviating the need for my offensive which would have secured it for our country."

"It disarms Germany completely, they hand back all the land they have taken in the present war and in the war of 1871, while Germany and Austria will be forever weakened by their non-German-speaking parts such as Poland and Czechoslovakia becoming sovereign nations."

"But we do not get the west bank of the Rhine which my offensive will achieve."

"That is so, but that will not be necessary for the defence of France. We have to live with the fact that there will always be seventy million Germans next door to us, and the British and the Americans have said they will guarantee our eastern frontier."

"Then this is not a peace. This is a ceasefire for the next twenty years. Nothing more. I could have delivered complete victory for our country, and this means I cannot. I confess I am not sure how this frustration of my ambitions will inform any future actions of mine."

I could see that the discussion between Clemenceau, Foch, and Pétain on what had been achieved might take some time, but Clemenceau brought matters to a sudden close. "Gentlemen, Parliament opens in ten minutes, and I will go there to announce victory. I would be grateful if you would come to witness my triumph."

We drove in convoy from the Elysée Palace to the French parliament, cheered by the masses who were already thronging the streets. Foch sat in the front car with Clemenceau and Mycroft while I sat with an infuriated Pétain. "It is indeed an honour," he said sourly, "to sit with the best-known associate of the great Mr Sherlock Holmes. But if I had been given the chance to launch my offensive, it would be I who would be in the front car."

Clemenceau made his victory address to the French assembly, and, as it drew to a close, Mycroft tugged at my sleeve, and whispered, "It is time we returned to London, Dr Watson."

If this were an adventure with Sherlock Holmes in the 1890s, my friend would now explain how he had achieved his results while he sat on the cushions of a first-class railway compartment speeding its way back to London. As it was, our journey from Paris to London was long and arduous, and most of what Mycroft told me was pronounced in railway trucks which in happier times would have been used for the transport of freight or livestock. But, as we sat on top of crates in one of a long succession of these, a rare smile played on Mycroft's lips.

"You ended your first work, *A Study in Scarlet*, by quoting the great Roman poet, Horace," he said to me. "I regard what you have just been witness to as my greatest if not my first triumph, and I too will quote that master of Latin verse. So I will say, 'Exegi monumentum.'"

"It is the last of Horace's *Odes* you are quoting from," I said, "and you are saying you have created a monument."

Mycroft smiled again.

"That is so. Perhaps it would help if I would explain my *modus operandi* in this matter, the result of which I cannot believe can be categorised as anything less than monumental."

"It would be as well for the record which I plan to create of your activities if you did that."

"Politics is, as Prince Otto von Bismark said, the art of the possible. In this case politics has been about getting people to agree to what they might not otherwise agree to. It is not necessary for the parties to agree for longer than a second to anything but once they have agreed it is very hard for them to back out. The trick in the matter to which you have just been witness was to get the parties to agree to matters that they would normally regard as unacceptable, which requires them to get something of what they want and to forgo other things that were close to their heart."

"Perhaps you could explain."

"In a British context, the power of patronage is strong. If you need to persuade someone of something they might not otherwise agree to, they can be offered an honour, or a senior position in government or in another body, or both. This is often sufficient to prompt a desired course of action."

"But here you were dealing with German and French politicians and military personnel to whom you were unable to offer anything like that."

"What you say is true but pointing out what a signature meant to each personally or the consequences to them personally of objecting to a signature had much the same effect."

"Are you able to more specific?"

"I was helped in the matter by Groener. You will recall, I asked what was in it for him and he said that he would get command of the German army after its defeat which was akin to being in charge of the German Reich. His extraordinarily convenient intervention enabled me to make the Kaiser aware of a possible trial for war-crimes. And Groener, who deserves a share of my victory palms, although he would be well-advised to keep a low profile after this, had even taken the trouble to make transport available to take the Kaiser into exile. The Kaiser's continued presence at the helm was a major obstacle to getting the Germans to agree to an armistice."

"So that was for whom the seventh car was?"

"Precisely so. I understand that the Kaiser has fled to the Netherlands. The formidable Dutch queen will doubtless be prepared to take one Prussian who is less than two metres foot tall, though no more. And she will use the same threats on the French as she did on the Germans to prevent the French from trying to capture him. Groener's intervention also enabled Hindenburg to avoid responsibility for the defeat of his nation.

Hindenburg could say that his hand had been forced by the politicians."

"And of course by Groener."

"That is so."

"Will it be seen as a stab in the back?"

Mycroft paused. "That may be the expression that is used in the future, although the Germans had been defeated in the field. Without Groener playing his cards as he did, the war might still be going on."

"And Erzberger?"

"A junior politician such as he is seeking no more than to climb the greasy pole of progression. Telling him that signing up to the Armistice terms was the way for him to make this progression was what persuaded him that that was the right thing to do. Just as persuading Foch that a failure to give Erzberger some minor concessions would mean that Pétain's offensive in the south would proceed. And then Pétain would get the main credit for the victory. That was the key to getting Foch to give the Germans more time to withdraw their forces."

By now, we were nearing London and a thought struck me, dredged from the depths of my memory of hours spent learning Latin, which seemed apposite to what I had been witness to.

"Does not Horace say in the poem you just quoted from, that the monument he has constructed will be more everlasting than bronze? Is that how you perceive the settlement you have achieved?"

Another rare smile.

"'Perenior aere,' in the original Latin. I am not sure that political settlements or indeed anything else can be more everlasting than bronze. What I have achieved will continue to keep the ship of the British state on an even keel although the chances of it staying there depend, as ever, on me remaining in post as... well, good Doctor, I think you have elsewhere described my role in government with your characteristic accuracy."

The Art of the Possible - Part 3 by Mycroft Holmes

Dr Watson and I eventually arrived in London on the afternoon of Tuesday the 12th of November. At Victoria we went our separate ways, and I headed straight to 10 Downing Street to debrief the Prime Minister.

When I got there, it was to find Mr Lloyd George pacing the floor in fury.

"Eleven o'clock! Eleven o'clock! The Armistice came into effect at a time which enabled Clemenceau to get all the credit for the victory himself," he said. "It was he who was the first leader to make a speech to his national assembly. Our Parliament here does not start sitting until the afternoon and we are an hour behind France so by the time I could stand before the House of Commons, the news was out, people had crowded onto the streets, and no one listened to what I had to say!"

"Prime Minister, even on the last day of the war, a thousand men were killed, wounded, or were reported missing every hour, so finishing the war at eleven o'clock European time rather than at three o'clock for an announcement to the House of Commons saved four thousand casualties. There was a better argument for finishing the war earlier than it did, and that would have been possible had Wemyss not come up with his eleventh hour on the eleventh day of the eleventh month formulation. That will have been a death warrant to thousands of men, although I am sure the expression Wemyss has coined will win him immortality."

Lloyd George continued to pace the floor.

"And we will have to accept the Fourteen Points, including the limitations they place on our freedom of action."

"Prime Minister," I soothed, "we are a great nation and will remain so no matter how events play out – unlike the French, the Germans, or the Russians. For all the words of goodwill in the Fourteen Points, once they or something like them are signed up to by the other belligerents, we can still pay as much notice as we wish to, and claim *force majeure* if we have a need to. The Points make no mention of *force majeure*, and we can always claim that it overrides any of them if we want to add secret protocols to treaties, blockade ports, or restrict trade."

"And I have agreed to guarantee France's eastern borders."

"I would refer you to my previous remark on the enforceability of that. I suspect the Americans would also refer you to my previous remark."

There was a long pause.

"How old are you, Mr Holmes?"

"I am seventy-one."

"I feel you are at your age maybe better suited to the role of a figurehead of the British Government than to being its main counsellor."

"I have never sought a fortune or an honour, Prime Minister. Neither a role as the head of a government organization nor a position in the House of Lords is of any appeal."

"Very well, we will have to see what your next commission shall be."

I was not the only person for whom agreement to the eleven o'clock timing for the start of the cease-fire had a negative impact on their career. Rosslyn Wemyss was moved from the position of First Sea Lord the following year. But this is not the place to air personal grievances, and I will not weary the reader with details of my own activities over the next few years other than to append the exchanges which follow which I had with two of the main figures in this record of events.

In August 1921, Matthias Erzberger, who had attained high office as Germany's post-war Finance Minister, was assassinated. No one had been brought to trial by the time of his funeral, but it was thought overwhelmingly likely that his murder had been committed by people who abhorred his role in the signing of the Armistice.

One of the roles Mr Lloyd George had given to me was to be at events where it was felt that Great Britain should be represented but it was not clear by whom – perhaps for me *being* the British government is a more difficult habit to give up than it is to acquire. So it was that it was I who represented the British government at Erzberger's funeral at Biberach in the south-western corner of Germany.

Among the attendees – for reasons that will become clear, I do not use the word "mourners" – was Wilhelm Groener.

He had, like me, been forced into a form of retirement, but said perkily, "I am pleased we were able to reach a solution three years ago, Mr Holmes, not that it seems to have done either of our careers much good. Although I suppose we are both better off than poor Erzberger. Still, I think I did my best to help him in his negotiations."

"It was a remarkable achievement," I opined cautiously, "to get seven fuelled cars together when Germany was out of everything."

"That is not what I was thinking of. It was the demand that we withdraw our troops across the Rhine in two weeks. As a railwayman, I knew two weeks gave us enough time to bring our troops back and then to hand our rolling stock to the French. But I said it could not be done in order to give Erzberger a chance to get something for his troubles."

I think Groener saw my look of surprise.

"German and Belgian infrastructure were largely undamaged," he explained, "our supply lines back to Germany were shorter than they had been for four years, and the distances involved were not so great. When troops arrived in Berlin, our Chancellor was able to say to them that they had returned undefeated at a time of our choosing, and to blame their withdrawal on the Kaiser." He paused and then added with a nod at Erzberger's coffin. "Not that the one concession that I managed to get poor Erzberger seems to have done him much good, but it did make the bitter pill of defeat slightly easier to swallow. And I got to be head of the army."

"You are a master of what can be achieved," said I, sensing once again a man with some of my own skills albeit one who whose motivation was personal ambition rather than good statecraft."

"I am sure that like you I will be back in a government role when my country needs a pragmatist," continued Groener, "and I will be at its service when it does so."

Even more perky was Paul von Hindenburg, who singled me out as someone whose ear he wanted to bend. "You will understand, Herr Holmes," said he, "that I am only here at the funeral of a former government minister for the sake of form. But if you are sent to represent your country in funerals in Germany, it can only be because you have fallen out of your government's favour."

"I remain at my country's service," I said warily.

"Politics, dear Herr Holmes, is the art of the possible. You may have won a battle five years ago," Hindenburg continued, "but I will win the war. It is only a question of awaiting the moment. I presented the surrender at Compiègne as a stab in the back for an army that was about to be victorious, and no one could prove me wrong."

"An army on the verge of victory," I commented, "is able to supply food to its people so that they do not revolt, supply weapons to its forces so that they do not mutiny, and has allies queueing up to join it rather than allies who are queueing up to sign surrender terms."

"Details, Herr Holmes," shrugged Hindenburg, "mere details. And unprovable. In some ways even the abominable Treaty of Versailles that finally ended the war has strengthened our hand as, to the east, rather than the formidable Russia and Austria-Hungary as our neighbours, we now have a number of weak and newly constituted countries."

A pause.

"Or we do for the moment," he added before he continued. "You know, I expect I will become President of Germany in a few years' time. Under our new constitution it is the president who decides who is to be our country's chancellor if there is a political stalemate. Let us see what will happen then. You would not be here representing your country if you were still in a position of influence with your government, whereas I have enhanced my power. And a British government without Mr Mycroft Holmes is an altogether less formidable foe for my country."

I fixed him with a stare, "As you say, Field Marshal, politics is truly the art of the possible. And I remain the master of it. If my country needs to become a more formidable foe to your country or any other, I am sure that I will once more be summoned to the colours. And I am always at the ready to answer my country's call."

Afterword by Henry Durham

One of the fascinations of these memoirs of Mycroft Holmes is the light they throw on the behaviour of the main players – not just at the time of the events described but sometimes also regarding events that happened years later.

So here we learn how Paul von Hindenburg was able to pass off a catastrophic defeat where he had been supreme commander of the German Imperial Army as a personal victory for him, and how the coining of the famous, "Eleventh hour, of the eleventh day, of the eleventh month," by Rosslyn Wemyss resulted in him being moved from his position as First Lord of the Admiralty. When he became German president, the last person Paul von Hindenburg elevated to the role of chancellor was Adolf Hitler.

Perhaps still chastened by not being the first leader to declare victory in 1918, Lloyd George, who had stood down from being British Prime in 1922, travelled to Germany twice to meet Hitler. The former British Prime Minister declared Hitler to be "one of the greatest men."

And perhaps most strikingly of all, here we learn why twenty-two years after the signing of the Armistice and the thwarting of his ambition to lead the final advance on the Germans, Marshal Pétain was prepared to act as Hitler's puppet in Vichy France. After meeting Hitler in October 1940, Pétain made a broadcast in which he said, "I have today entered into the way of collaboration."

Marshal Pétain, a true French hero of the First World War, ended his days in prison for this collaboration.

EPISODE V

The Royal Bachelor - Part 1 by Mycroft Holmes

Perhaps the strange thing is that the Royals are not odder. And that some are not odd at all.

It is the fate of most people to have odd ancestors but the effect of them is mitigated by miscegenation with people whose ancestors had different oddities. Royal families, by contrast, only marry each other, and so the chances of oddities being accentuated are greatly increased.

Let us consider the ancestry of Queen's Victoria's eldest son who was to become Edward VII.

The behaviour of Victoria's paternal grandfather, George III, was so erratic, that he had to be the subject of physical restraint, and a regent appointed in his place. Edward VII's father was Prince Albert, whose maternal grandfather, Augustus, Duke of Saxe-Gotha-Altenburg, wore women's clothes at court, dyed his hair a different colour each day, and insisted courtiers called him Emilie.

And Victoria and Albert, Edward VII's parents, were first cousins.

It is perhaps no wonder that their eldest son frolicked from scandal to scandal, and that his eldest son, Albert Victor, did the same. Both were habitués of places of ill repute and engaged in behaviour of a decadence redolent of the worst excesses of Imperial Rome. It was only his early death from influenza that prevented Albert Victor becoming king after Edward VII.

And yet, as though stability in the royal house were the will of fate, the next in line after Albert Victor was the notably austere George, the second of Edward VII's six children by his wife, Queen Alexandra of Denmark. George V ascended the throne in 1910 and in his turn, George V had six children. King George V's death occurred in January 1936 after a reign spanning a quarter of a century. He had been in poor health for several years and had been thought to be on his way out of this life on a number of previous occasions before unexpectedly rallying. I have never understood the popular fascination in the lives of our royals and, although I fulfilled my invitation to Westminster Abbey for the funeral, the event was of little moment to me. He was succeeded on the throne by his eldest son who adopted the name Edward on his ascent to the throne and was due to be crowned Edward VIII in 1937.

The matter that follows saw me called back to the service of my country at the age of eighty-eight. My reader should be aware that I am seven years older than my brother Sherlock and so was already seventy-one when the Great War came to its end. Unlike my brother who had betaken himself to the Sussex coast long before that conflagration began, I remained in London dividing my time between my quarters in Pall Mall and the Diogenes Club.

147

So it was that on the morning of the 15th of November of 1936 that I stood at the window of my quarters and surveyed the passers-by. The demeanour of one figure on the other side of the road caught my eye. Dressed in military uniform, he stood on the pavement in a paroxysm of uncertainty as he peeped up in a nervous, hesitating fashion at my windows while his body oscillated backward and forward, and his fingers fidgeted nervously at his glove buttons. Suddenly, with a plunge, as of the swimmer who leaves the bank, he hurried across the road, weaving an unsteady way through the speeding traffic. Seconds later came the sharp clang of the bell.

As my brother has commented, standing wracked with prevarication upon the pavement always means some *affaire de cœur*. My petitioner wanted to have some advice, but was not sure if the matter was not perhaps too delicate for communication. When he entered, the moustachioed forty-year-old stood for a while as though unsure of what to do next. Several times he opened his mouth to speak and then stopped as though what he had to say required too much of him. Unlike my brother, Sherlock, I have neither a fellow dweller in my lodgings nor any expectation of petitioners, so my sitting room only sits one. In the end I let my visitor sit in my seat and I took my station at the window facing into the room.

Alec Hardinge

1894 - 1960

"My name is Alec Hardinge," my visitor eventually said. "I am the personal secretary of King Edward VIII." There was another long pause. "I confess I find my role difficult at the best of times without having to engage in behaviour which has all the hallmarks of being treasonous," he continued, grinding out this last sentence out as though in explanation of his inability to speak.

It was only after Hardinge had lit his pipe and taken several soothing gulps from it that he was able to give any further expression to his thoughts and, even then, what I set out below reflects a delivery interrupted by long pauses.

"It's like this. Our monarch and my master, Edward VIII, has been King since January of this year. Before he ascended the throne, he consorted with a string of women who were married to someone else – much like his grandfather did – but this was of no great significance as there seemed no good reason why he should be the first Prince of Wales not to have a mistress. But as King, he is expected to marry someone of royal blood and to provide this country with an heir."

The matters of the heart which Hardinge referred to seemed to be rather out of the ambit of where I might be able to help the King's secretary, but I forbore to interrupt him.

"And on whom do you think his eyes have lighted as his bride?" asked Hardinge eventually.

I confess it is not my habit to follow the activities of this country's royalty and nobility in the popular press, so I felt I had nothing to say. I am in any case not enamoured of guessing games.

"She is an American," said the Hardinge.

"There is surely no objection to that in this new meritocratic world," I uttered, finally making a reply in the hope of getting my interlocutor to the point. As I awaited his next remark, I recalled the trivial matter the good Dr Watson narrated under the title *The Noble Bachelor* on the planned marriage of the son of one of our most our noble houses with an American lady – a union which would have improved the financial fortunes of this older but poorer side of the Atlantic and the breeding stock of a *nouveau riche* family on that ocean's other shore. In truth, I wondered if the nationality of the King's paramour could really be all that that was on Hardinge's mind, and reflected that, unusually, this consultation might be even more facile than the disquisitions often put before my brother.

"Indeed," said Hardinge at last, "in these..." he paused as he sought the right word, "...egalitarian times, that is undoubtedly so. The problem is that like the rest of His Royal Highness's string of mistresses, the King's present mistress, Mrs Simpson, is already married to someone else. And she was married to someone else before that."

"Surely the whole point of being King is that you can have whatever and whomever you want."

"The King is the head of the Anglican church and must be expected to follow its rules. The Anglican church will not allow divorcees to remarry under its roof while the victim of the divorce is still alive," replied Hardinge somewhat primly.

"He is also the head of the Scottish church so his position as head of any church can have no more than ceremonial significance," was my riposte.

"The Scottish Church will not allow divorcees to remarry under its roof either."

"The Anglican church was founded to let a divorced man remarry under its auspices. Surely it can see its way to waiving any objections it may have to the King's proposed union."

"Henry VIII was never divorced," replied Hardinge, slightly defensively to my jibing response. "He was widowed by Jane Seymour, he left Catherine Parr a widow, and he had four marriages that were annulled, so no marriage had in fact taken place. And hence there was no obstacle to him being married in church."

"Yet Anne Boleyn and Catherine Howard were executed for adultery. From what you say, they betrayed a marriage that had never actually occurred."

"I do not think anyone saw fit to draw Henry VIII's attention to this logical inconsistency at the time. And we are talking of events that happened four-hundred years ago. My focus is on the here and now."

"Would it not be easiest if the Church of England were simply prevailed upon to annul the present marriage of the King's paramour?"

"The solution you propose has been considered and it would enable the King to marry a woman who had not previously been married. But Mr Simpson is already Mrs Simpson's second husband."

"Could the Church of England not annul the first marriage as well?"

"To have the King marry someone who would have had two previous marriage annulments – which would both be recent and in the public domain – would be seen as perhaps a little too convenient."

"Might not," I ventured, not entirely sure whether I should ask the question at all or couch it in the form that follows, "the lives of Mrs Simpson's two previous husbands come to an unexpected and premature end? There could be no objection to the King marrying a woman who had been twice widowed."

"That option has of course also been considered but one of her previous husbands lives in the United States where such matters are more difficult to arrange for the British government. And the sudden and premature death of two men who had been married to a woman whom the King subsequently married might give rise to awkward questions."

I was astonished to see how far the matter had got and sat in thought for a few moments. In the end I asked, "So, what would you like me to do, Mr Hardinge?"

"The Prime Minister has asked me to sound you out on whether you would be prepared to find a way to resolve the impasse."

"So, you are acting as a messenger for the Prime Minister on this matter? Is that a fitting role for someone who is supposed to be the King's secretary?"

Hardinge shifted uneasily and looked into the distance.

"If you agree to act, the Prime Minister, Mr Baldwin, and the Archbishop of Canterbury, Cosmo Gordon Lang, will see you in Downing Street at eleven o'clock this morning."

I had some misgivings about prosecuting the matter Hardinge had brought to my attention. Indeed, had the matter been brought under the purview of some more junior member of the government – the Lord Chancellor or the Home Secretary, for example – I might have let it pass. As it was, I felt I could hardly decline to act. A look of relief crossed Hardinge's face when I expressed my consent, and he was soon on his way. As I strode up Pall Mall and through Whitehall towards Downing Street a few minutes later, I felt there were three options to solve the impasse:

❖ The Church of England might be persuaded to waive its objections to this marriage; or
❖ The King might be persuaded to give up his desire to make Mrs Simpson his choice of bride; or
❖ In the event of the failure of both of the first two options, the King would have to abdicate.

Stanley Baldwin

1867 - 1947

Cosmo Lang

1864 - 1945

The sixty-nine-year-old Baldwin was in his third term as Prime Minister, but these terms had not been consecutive, and he was widely regarded as no more than a pair of hands to whom the seals of office could be safely entrusted in the absence of some more inspirational leader. This grey image was mirrored in a grey appearance and grey dress. The seventy-two-year-old archbishop, also soberly attired, was in every sense as grey as the Prime Minister, and bore an air of the driest asceticism.

I put to the two of them the King's desire to marry Mrs Simpson, and asked them to state their objections.

"It is the duty and the honour of the holder of my office," replied Lang in a melodious Scottish accent, "to place the crown on the head of the occupant of the British throne. Of the citizens on this planet, nearly one in four will have the joy of regarding that occupant of the throne as their sovereign. They have a right to expect a higher standard of behaviour from the monarch of Great Britain than if they were citizens of some lesser country. Our monarch has from God received a high and sacred trust. If he follows his wishes as you have outlined them, he will have surrendered that trust, and by extension surrendered the trust of the Empire's citizens. Accordingly, I fear that if the King is accommodated in his wish to marry a woman who will have been twice divorced, I will have to find some excuse not to perform his coronation, which is due to take place next year."

"We have a line to hold across the Empire," chimed in Baldwin. "Country after country is agitating for independence. Perceived moral decadence in this country will only fuel the flames of that. If we cannot provide a moral example to the Empire, then it will wither away. You must persuade the King it is his duty not to marry a divorced woman. I have arranged for you to see him at his quarters in Windsor tomorrow. As a King he is of course inaccessible on the side of honour or material reward but as Prime Minister – and I am sure the Archbishop is in accord with what I will say now – you have my authority to agree with him any sort of *modus vivendi* with regard to Mrs Simpson short of marriage."

"And what is your impression of the King?" I asked.

"He is an abnormal being – half child, half genius," said Baldwin. "It is as though two or three cells in his brain have remained entirely undeveloped, whilst the rest of him is a mature man. He is not a thinker. He takes his ideas from the daily press instead of thinking things out for himself. He conducts no serious reading – none at all. It is thus very difficult to reason with him in any way. I wish you more success than I or the Archbishop have had."

The King's residence on the Windsor estate is called Fort Belvedere. Originally built in the early nineteenth century as a folly, it was constructed on top of a hill. Even from ground level, it has commanding views over the surrounding countryside, and it is supposed to be possible to see seven counties from its tower. I was bidden to wait in an airy drawing-room with double-doors.

At precisely eleven o'clock, the time of the appointment, a uniformed doorman swung open the doors. But, rather than heralding the arrival of the King, this action merely acted as a prelude to the air filling with the sound of the bagpipe.

Edward VIII appeared standing to one side of the doors, dressed in a kilt, and, as he blew down the pipe of the instrument to make the tune, and squeezed the bag with his arm to create the drone, the effort made his face go brick-red. A lady, who I could only assume was Mrs Simpson, came through the door and sat down opposite me. It was only once she was seated on a settee,

Edward VIII
1894 -1972

Wallace Simpson
1896 - 1986

that His Majesty sat down beside her with his bagpipe rested on the cushion on the other side.

I had expected Mrs Simpson to be young, dashing, and beautiful. Indeed, I had anticipated that it would require the pen of the good Dr Watson, who brought to life the beauty of women such as Irene Adler and Hattie Duran, to do her full justice. But, while she was a good-looking woman, slim almost thin, and elegantly dressed, Mrs Simpson looked almost the same age as the forty-two-year-old King. I confess, even though such considerations are well outside the area where I had hitherto been asked to supply expertise, I found it hard to imagine why a man might become so besotted by her that there might be discussion about him sacrificing his kingdom for her hand.

Although the King's appointment was with me, he first of all turned to address Mrs Simpson.

"What did you think of my performance, my dear?"

"It was magnificent. Powerful and stirring. The command you display over your instrument is masterful."

"I am as ever inspired by you."

"You say too much, my dearest," said Mrs Simpson, simpering slightly.

The King turned a steady eye on me, "So Mr Holmes, you are the latest emissary from those twin authorities on morality – the government and the Church of England. They have separately and together tried to dissuade me from my intention to marry Mrs Simpson."

"Your Majesty," I asked, "is that your settled intent?"

"It is."

"You are aware, Your Majesty, that if you attempt to go through with this, you will cause a constitutional crisis. The government will probably fall, dominions will seek to leave the Empire, and there is no knowing where matters might end."

The King looked into the distance. "I cannot pretend to anyone and certainly not to you, Mr Holmes, that I would be able to carry the heavy burden of responsibility and to discharge the sacred duties of the monarch in a way that I would wish without the support of the woman I love. Is there not a saying, 'Justice though the heavens fall'? My love for Mrs Simpson is such, that I would be prepared to let the heavens fall to have her as my bride."

"But," I countered, "there is nothing to preclude you having Mrs Simpson at your side. It would be perfectly possible for you to have an arrangement whereby you could see her whenever you wished. It would not be difficult to find a bride of a suitable background who would accommodate your regular absences. Queen Alexandra, your grandfather's wife, was aware of her husband's myriad infidelities…."

The King grinned and said, "When my grandfather died, my grandmother is supposed to have said, 'For once I know where he is lying tonight,'"

"I know that such a thing will never happen with you, my dear," interjected Mrs Simpson.

"…and accepted them," I continued, ignoring the interruptions from the couple, "as a normal part of being a royal consort. She was of course a Danish princess and so was used to the requirements of being a royal consort. Such an attitude of mind is perhaps particular to people with a royal background."

"So you are saying to me, Mr Holmes," replied the King, "that the government and the church would rather I had Mrs Simpson as a permanent royal mistress than that I live with her in the bonds of matrimony?"

"I fear that is so."

"Mr Holmes, I am sure you have done plenty of research into me and you will know something of my history."

I felt it would be unwise to say anything at all and so I held my counsel.

"Has your research ever caused you to wonder why I have always preferred the company of married women who in turn have remained in wedlock?"

Again, I felt it was wiser not to make a comment which would denote I had undertaken any sort of speculation on what I regarded as something of a moot point.

"I was introduced to Mrs Simpson by a Mrs Thelma Furness. She was my then royal companion and was the wife of one of my noblemen. Before that I consorted with a Mrs Freda Dudley Ward, the wife of a Liberal Member of Parliament."

"I have no doubt," I said at length, "that my brother, Sherlock, would deduce a reason for this preference of yours for the company of married women, perhaps from an observation of some trifling feature of your person, Your Majesty, but I fear that that is not…"

Paying no heed to me, the King stood up and once more took up his bagpipes.

He strode up and down the room, playing the same air that he had played to accompany Mrs Simpson at her first entrance. In the confined space the sound of the pipes had almost deafened me by the time he had sat down, again brick-red in the face, and once more taken his place with his bagpipes on the sofa on one side of him and Mrs Simpson on the other.

"I myself wrote that air for Mrs Simpson," he said, as though to explain himself.

I think he was expecting a question from me, but I said nothing so eventually he continued.

"I practised it on the bagpipes at Balmoral so much that in the end my father ordered me to stop playing. And he subsequently told me, he would forbid me to marry her in his lifetime which was a power he had over me as I needed to obtain his consent for any wife that I took."

He looked at me, again as if expecting a question but I said nothing, so he continued.

"I had played this instrument," he patted the bag of his instrument, "as a youth. But it was Mrs Simpson who rekindled my powers with it" – he nodded vaguely downwards – "in a way that other women could not."

"It was a simple thing, my dear," said Mrs Simpson, blushing slightly, "and I am not sure that Mr H – "

"My preference for married women is explained by the fact that my instrument was," the king paused as he considered his next words and he ran his hand over his instrument again, "deficient – whether in the pipe or in the sack I would not wish to specify – but in a way that is difficult for a man to express. And," he added, "the reason why my previous companions stayed in their marriages was to ensure that they had some consortium with their husbands. And it is Mrs Simpson – "

"My dearest, are you sure you wish to explore this?"

"– to whom I owe the restoration of my instrument's prowess," the King again glanced downwards. "And that is why I have foresworn all others to marry her, although she is at present married to another. And that is why I cannot be on the throne without Mrs Simpson's support."

"But Mrs Simpson's support is what I am offering you," I said at last, unable to understand why the King was unable to see that the offer I was making gave him precisely what he wanted.

"You are suggesting that the Church of England has moral scruples about me marrying Mrs Simpson. But it apparently has none about me having a sham marriage to some royal of whom I will be probably a close blood relative, at the same time as I have a mistress with whom I spend all my time apart from when my wife and I are required to be seen together at ceremonial occasions."

"It is you who have put it in those precise terms. But what you say is what the government and the church are prepared to countenance if you assent."

"I consider the proposal you suggest indecent and will never accept it."

"In spite of the possible consequences for the country, the Empire, and the Crown?"

"Governments come and governments go. If the government must change to give me a Prime Minister who will allow me to fulfil my destiny, then so be it."

It had not been my intention to talk to Mrs Simpson at all but, given the King's apparently unshakeable desire to marry her, I felt obliged to ask her what she made of the situation.

"The man who seeks my hand in marriage is a King," she replied. "It is, in spite of everything, difficult to disoblige a King."

"And would you be prepared to accommodate the arrangement that I have suggested on the government's behalf?"

"It is, in spite of everything, difficult to disoblige a King," she repeated serenely.

I was soon back in London where I reported back to Baldwin. I do not think that he was surprised when I gave him the King's response. "When I was a little boy in Worcestershire reading history books, I never thought I should have to interfere between a king and his mistress," he mused to me.

"I take it that if the King persists in his ambition to marry Mrs Simpson, your wish would be for him to be removed from the throne with the minimum of fuss."

"My preferred option would be what we have offered him. Since that has been rejected so far, we will need to look at ways of removing him from the throne."

"Would you like me to see if he might be persuaded to go quietly?"

"It would be my greatest wish."

I repaired to my quarters and considered the options.

The last king to be toppled was James II who fled when the army of William of Orange landed in Devonshire in 1688. The cause of this invasion had been the birth of a son to the Roman Catholic King James and his wife. Many suspected this son had been an imposter who had been smuggled into the palace. The last removal of a sitting monarch from a position of power had been in 1811 when the future George IV had been appointed as regent for his father George III.

A recommendation from me that a foreign army should land in England to dethrone the king could not, I felt, be categorised as persuading him to go quietly, and it would be difficult to sustain the argument that Edward VIII was insane while he was alive to defend himself of the charge. If, on the other hand, I mused, evidence could be found that the King was not the legitimate incumbent of the throne, then maybe he could be side-lined. But what I needed was evidence or perhaps, to be more precise, material on which a particular construction could be placed. This idea and others swirled through my head as I considered how I might move.

My brother has described the literary ideas of the good Dr Watson as exceedingly pertinacious. Sherlock wrote of this when he eventually agreed to chronicle one of his own trivial adventures rather than leaving the job to Dr Watson. My brother saw it as his duty to avoid pandering to popular taste and to confine himself rigidly to facts and figures. He commented, having taken pen in hand, that it was only at this moment of creation that he began to realise that the matter must be presented in such a way as may interest the reader.

I do not propose that the matters I relate here should be read until many years after my death and even then only as an academic textbook on statecraft. Nevertheless, I find it impossible to resist the temptation – my brother's comment on the pertinacity of Dr Watson's ideas is unusually perceptive by his standards – to write a conclusion to these matters in any style other than in that of a penny-dreadful tale of suspense. I fear my academic reader of this text in the distant future will have to forgive this lapse from the lofty and rigorous standards I seek to set. I also note my brother's comment in *The Blanched Soldier* on the usefulness of having a biographer to whom any development comes as a perpetual surprise, and to whom the future is always a closed book. It was by concealing such links in the chain that Dr Watson was able to produce his meretricious finales. I have no such biographer, so my reader must forgive me if this narrative only discloses some of the cards in my hand as I play them.

I have left the next few paragraphs to Dr Watson to pen in his inimitable style.

The Royal Bachelor – Part 2 by Dr Watson

It was the best of times once more as my friend, Mr Sherlock Holmes, of whom I had seen so little in recent years, stood at my door.

"We will shortly be joined by my brother, Mycroft, who has a brief he did not disclose on the telegram he sent this afternoon," said Sherlock Holmes.

While experience had taught me to be wary of commissions from Mycroft Holmes, my joy at seeing my friend drove any forebodings from my mind. We had done no more than light our pipes when Mycroft arrived.

"It is not too much to say," started Mycroft, "that the future of this country and its Empire could rest on the satisfactory resolution of the matter I am about to put before you."

"Pray continue," said his younger brother.

"There is a plot to discredit our King before his coronation next year."

"What form will this plot take?"

"The Royal Physician has always been an honorary title. The current office-holder, Lord Dawson of Penn, has said he wants to be paid what will be a substantial sum to continue in his role."

"Surely another physician could be found?"

"That is so, except that Lord Dawson has some leverage over us. He claims to have evidence that will call into question the legitimacy of the last king."

"Could you expand on what you have just said."

"George V's father, Edward VII, had a colourful love life. Lord Penn has suggested that his wife, Queen Alexandra, sought solace in another man's arms, and that George V's natural father was not the man to whom she was married."

"But that would call into question the ascent to the throne of the present King."

"Quite so. The constitutional implications could hardly be more profound."

"But is it true?"

"The damage that a plausible accusation to this effect would cause is such that it would be better to eliminate the evidence rather than seek to establish whether the accusation is true. That is why I need an expert in breaking and entering to gain access to the Royal Physician's medical records, and a man with a medical background to identify what to take."

"You want me to break and enter the practice of the Royal Physician?" and as he asked this question of his brother, my friend sounded aghast.

"And you want me to assist in the abstraction of the medical records of a member of the royal family?" I asked, similarly shocked.

"Both of you can be relied upon to take your secrets to the grave. And for both of you that trip to the grave cannot be all that far off," replied Mycroft austerely. "You, Sherlock, have an unparalleled record of breaking, entering, and making good your escape whether it be in Kensington, Hampstead, or Brixton. And you, Doctor Watson, will never have got closer to a practice in Harley Street than you will at this juncture."

I have commented elsewhere that my friend is accessible on the side of flattery and once he had, rather grudgingly, assented to Mycroft's request I felt it would be ill-advised of me not lend my support. And so it was on the evening of 27 November 1936 that

Sherlock Holmes and I stood on the Harley Street doorstep of Lord Dawson.

In the *Bruce-Partington Plans* of 1895, Holmes and I had leapt down from the street into the area to gain access through the basement to the Kensington house of Steiner, the German spy, at 13 Caulfield Gardens. Forty years later by contrast, we were relieved to find the area could be accessed by a flight of steps to which the gate was unlocked. While the years may have impaired our agility, they had not had any effect on the resourcefulness of Sherlock Holmes, and a few minutes later he had cut a circle of glass out of a door, lifted the latch, and we were inside the Royal Physician's practice.

As might be expected, the records within the doctor's archives were both methodically and securely stored, but the robust security measures Lord Dawson had taken were as putty when confronted by the prowess of my friend. Between us, we ransacked the place and took all the records we could find relating to George V – anything from detailed medical notes on him to diary entries which mentioned him and a lot more besides. As we exited through the front door. Holmes stooped to pick up a piece of paper which someone had pushed under it. On this was scrawled, "Lord Dawson of Penn, Killed many men, And that's why we sing, 'God Save the King!'"

"You have done very well," said Mycroft. "And you have done it with a lack of drama that is quite uncharacteristic of you. I shall sift through all the evidence you have provided and decide what to do."

And with that I returned with Sherlock Holmes to my practice in Queen Square.

The Royal Bachelor - Part 3 by Mycroft Holmes

I had a few other matters that needed organizing and it was not until the afternoon of Wednesday the 9th of December 1936 that I felt I had matters sufficiently in hand that I could make my way to Downing Street and make the final arrangements to proceed.

"I would ask you, Prime Minister," said I, as I sat before him, "to make an appointment for this evening at Fort Belvedere with the King."

"I am sure," replied Mr Baldwin, "that that could be arranged, but would you care to brief me on what you propose the meeting should cover?"

"You must leave matters entirely in my hands, Prime Minister. But I would ask that you also ask the King's three brothers to join us."

"I am sure that that too can be arranged. At what time would you wish this meeting?"

"I would like two cars to take you and me to arrive at half-past nine. And I would like the three princes to arrive in a motorcade with lights and sirens precisely fifteen minutes later – so at a quarter-to-ten."

"Why do we require two cars for our own party arriving at half-past-nine?"

"You must, I repeat, leave this matter in my hands. You and I will be in the first car. In the second car, we will have the King's Secretary, Mr Hardinge, and another person whose identity I cannot disclose to you but who, like Mr Hardinge, will be admitted to Fort Belvedere without question."

"And do we require lights and sirens for our own party?"

"Indeed not, Prime Minister. The arrival of our party, though not its complete makeup, will have been announced at Fort Belvedere and the house's occupants will have formed their own view on why the Prime Minister is paying a call. I would advise you that they may be in for a few surprises one of which will be the second arrival for which they will have received no notice of any sort."

Eight o'clock saw my party leave Downing Street in two cars as appointed. We – the Prime Minister and I in the first car – and the other two personages in the second, drove west through the busy London streets until the lights and bustle were behind us. Soon the headlights from our cars provided the only illumination on the narrow hedge-lined roads. On arrival at Fort Belvedere, the Prime Minister and I were shown into the same drawing-room I had sat in on my first visit. I had asked for a table to be set out in the middle of it, and Mr Baldwin and I sat on one side of it, while the King and his paramour sat on the other.

"I take it," began the King, "that you have come here to ask me to abdicate the throne."

"I am here," said Mr Baldwin, as I had briefed him, "to inform you, with regret, that I am unable to offer you an accommodation that would allow you to remain on the throne and to have Mrs

Simpson as your bride. I must request that either you forsake your wish to have her as your wife, although there is no obstacle to you retaining her as your mistress, or that you abdicate the throne, at which point you may do as you wish with her. If you abdicate, I can assure you that you may do so with honour and that ample financial provision will be made to you."

The King turned to Mrs Simpson.

"What do you think, Wallis?"

"My dear, this must be your decision," replied she in a voice of aching sweetness. "But you must find out the details of any settlement. You know I have always said one cannot be too thin or have too much money. But it is an unconscionably late hour to have this meeting and you know I will do nothing to disoblige my King and betrothed. So why not let us have a night's rest to think on it?"

"If I may interject," said I, "this matter must be brought to a head. It is the talk of America and while it is not a topic the British press has discussed to date, that forbearance cannot be relied upon forever. It cannot be drawn out any further." I fixed my gaze on the King. "Your Majesty will not be unaware of my own powers as an investigator and a document with the following text has come into my hand from unimpeachable sources. I shall read it out to you. It is a diary, and it is dated the 20th of January of this year – so the date of your father's death.

'At about 11 o'clock in the evening it was evident that the last stage of King's life might endure for many hours, unknown to the patient but little comporting with that dignity and serenity which he so richly merited, and which demanded a brief final scene. Hours of waiting just for the mechanical end when all that is really life has departed only exhausts the onlookers and keeps them so strained that they cannot avail themselves of the solace of thought, communion, or prayer. I therefore decided to determine the end and injected myself three quarters of a grain of morphia and shortly afterwards one tenth of a grain of cocaine into the distended jugular vein. In about a quarter of an hour – breathing quieter, appearance more placid, the physical struggle went as the King parted from this life.'"

The King turned white.

"What are you insinuating? That text is not from my hand."

"It is not but I cannot believe that its writer would have acted in this way without some authority from another party, and that other party could only have been you."

"It is a foul lie."

"If you say so. I am candidly unable to prove it. But if you do not abdicate, there will be an investigation into your predecessor's death, and I will be unable to control what findings it might have. Or what else it might uncover about you."

"And you have no witness and no means of substantiating your accusation," said the King, though he looked shaken to the core as he said it.

At that instant there was a tap on the door. The King was in no state to answer, so I said, "Come!"

The door opened and Hardinge came in escorting a lady in a white nurse's uniform with a raven-coloured lock of hair protruding from under her veil. "I understand, Your Maj – " began she in a soft Irish accent.

But she was interrupted by a gasp of unalloyed horror from the King over whose face appeared a look of supreme anguish.

"No, Your Majesty, no!" she cried as she looked wild-eyed around at the assembled company. "I swear I did not fulfil your request. As I told you I could not. And I swear I have said nothing to anyone about it as I told you I would not. Nothing at all."

"But you have said something now," I cut in, "and," I added looking to the window, "I can see the flash of police lights through the curtains as cars approach the building," although my remark was, in truth, unnecessary as we could also hear the eerie wail of police sirens as the vehicles drew up on the gravel outside.

"I will abdicate, I will abdicate," said the King in some panic. "I take it that with this…," he paused to find the right word, "ambush, you will have brought a deed of abdication with you for me to sign."

"Indeed so," I said smoothly, "I have it here," I fished the document I had prepared out of my brief- case before presenting it to the King along with a pen. "And your three brothers," I added, as the trio of princes filed into the room, "have just arrived to witness it. It is a happy chance for what we are doing that they have come with a police escort."

It took no more than a few seconds before the King had signed the deed, and his brothers had witnessed it. In a few seconds more Baldwin and I were back in our car heading to London.

"Where did you get that diary?" Baldwin asked, as the engine of the car purred into life.

"It is not quite a diary but rather the first draft of the memoirs of Lord Dawson of Penn. And it was he who administered the lethal injection that ended George V's life."

"And how did you get hold of that?"

"Two of my most trusted agents abstracted it. I fear I can say no more."

Catherine Black

1878 - 1949

"And who was the lady who came into the drawing room?"

"I had had her brought here on the pretext that the King had specifically asked that it be she who administer a sleeping draught to him. She is Nurse Catherine Black. She was the royal nurse. Alongside Lord Dawson, it was she who tended to the late George V during his final illness."

"But it was not she who administered the fatal injection?"

"I do not think so unless in spite of her denial she acted on the former King Edward's word. But the King Edward was not to know that, and I thought she was more likely to disclose whatever part she had had in the matter than Lord Dawson would have been. And, in any case, I thought that if anyone were to be prevailed upon by Edward to administer the *coup de grâce* to his father, he would regard her as more biddable than Lord Dawson. At my instigation, the arrival of black mariahs with sirens and lights outside the house of the King occurred at the instant when both she and he were at their most suggestible. You saw that my instinct was right, and it was her testimony that finally forced Edward's hand."

"What was his incentive for doing away with his father?"

"His father was empowered to ban him from marrying Mrs Simpson in his lifetime and had done so. But George V had no power over his son once he had died. George had also recovered from life-threatening conditions before, and so, while he was alive he posed an insurmountable obstacle to Edward's plans to marry Mrs Simpson."

"So was a crime in fact committed? Whoever performed the injections may only have shortened the life of George V's life by the briefest span."

"'May' I think is the key word. Lord Dawson was taking more responsibility than almost any of us would and, I would posit, more responsibility than was legal, in bringing King George V's life to a premature end however short a time he may have reduced it by."

"But was Lord Dawson acting on the Edward's instructions?"

"Having failed to persuade Nurse Black to administer a fatal injection, I would be surprised if the King did not try his luck with Lord Dawson, but we will now almost certainly never find out the truth. Dawson makes no mention of a request from the former King Edward in his memoirs, and it is highly unlikely that either party would ever be prepared to disclose it."

"But do Dawson's memoirs give any indication of whether he had any other motive for doing what he did?"

"I forbore to read out the rest of Lord Dawson's account of events as the considerations he gave for taking the actions that he did as, had I done so, they manifestly could not have been those of Nurse Black."

"And they were?"

"Besides what he wrote about not wishing the end to be drawn out, he added that he wanted George V's death to be announced in *The Times* in the morning rather than in the less serious press of the evening."

"And that was all?"

"Yes, that was all."

"And what should happen now?"

"I think a generous settlement for the former King Edward should be made but its payment should be conditional on him keeping a low profile. If he should prove in any way to be a nuisance, a delay in remitting funds to him will bring him and Mrs Simpson to their senses."

"And for Lord Dawson of Penn?"

"I am not, I think, the only person to wonder about the suddenness of George V's death and a scandalous verse is doing the popular rounds. My agents found a copy of it pushed under Lord Dawson's door. With the wide currency it has achieved, I do not imagine the damage to Lord Dawson's reputation will go away. You may find it useful both for controlling the next king and for controlling Lord Dawson that the latter remains in his current role as royal physician. If you do that, the next king will be wary of his doctor and his doctor will know that we have abstracted data about him which may be used against him."

"And Hardinge?"

"He should be given an honour for significantly exceeding what might be regarded as his responsibility. And he should be encouraged to act as the secretary of the new King, George VI, so that new incumbent of the throne knows his actions are always under scrutiny. As I recall, the new King has a young daughter, Elizabeth. She is still no more than ten years old, but I have already heard that she is possessed of wisdom rare in someone of her age. I see it as my duty to do everything in my powers to ensure that it is she who eventually inherits the throne. But now I see the first lights of London in the distance, and I would bid our driver to bring me to my Pall Mall quarters with all due speed."

Afterword by Henry Durham

After the shocks and outrages of this first book of Mycroftian memoirs spanning nearly four decades, the image of him bidding his driver to hasten to London so that he can return to the peace and solitude of his Pall Mall quarters is a reassuring one.

The events and main players of *The Royal Bachelor* are well enough known not to need further elaboration here, but it is perhaps worth dwelling on how Mycroft Holmes came to display such skill in manipulating people. We saw this with Kaiser Wilhelm and Foch in the previous episode and Edward VIII and his brother, Sherlock, here. As he presents himself in these memoirs, Mycroft Holmes knows for each person what button to press to get the desired effect.

When Sherlock Holmes first spoke of Mycroft Holmes to Watson in *The Greek Interpreter*, he mentioned that Mycroft had an extraordinary faculty for figures and audited some of the accounts of government departments. *The Greek Interpreter* took place in the late 1880s, and at that time adding up was a highly skilled human process as there was no mechanical means to facilitate it.

This all changed in 1887 with the invention of the comptometer (pictured left), an early and bulky version of the calculator. This new machine suddenly transformed the task of adding up long columns of figures from a rigorous intellectual exercise to a process of accurate punching.

The arrival of the comptometer will, on the face of it, have deskilled much of Mycroft's work as an auditor. And yet, is it a step too far to observe a parallel between the comptometer, which provided the right answer when the right buttons were pressed, and Mycroft Holmes applying its principles to pressing the right buttons to get the response he wanted from the people he dealt with?

In any event, the extraordinary faculty Mycroft had with numbers was something he was able to carry over to his dealings with the most eminent figures of his day for he seems to have known exactly the right button to press with all of them.

And there will be more of this to come in the next edition of his memoirs.

Henry Durham

London 2023

Milton Keynes UK
Ingram Content Group UK Ltd.
UKHW022124201123
432954UK00005B/177